and the
Land of the Midnight Sun

Emily Windsnap

and the
Land of the Midnight Sun

LIZ KESSLER

Illustrations by Natacha Ledwidge

Orion
Children's Books

First published in Great Britain in 2012
by Orion Children's Books
a division of the Orion Publishing Group Ltd
Orion House
5 Upper St Martin's Lane
London WC2H 9EA
An Hachette UK company

1 3 5 7 9 10 8 6 4 2

A catalogue record for this book is
available from the British Library.

ISBN 978 1 4440 0350 5

Printed in Great Britain by Clays Ltd, St Ives plc

This book is dedicated to my totally amazing agent, Catherine Clarke, to say thank you for ten years of being a wonderful support, advocate, friend, sounding board and the other hundred and one things you are. And for being the first step on the road to Emily ever making it out into the world. Thank you. Please don't ever retire.

The Return of the Mountain King

I have been dead, I have been lost,
I have been turned to rock and stone.

I have been ice, I have been fire,
I have been all, and some, and none.

I have been one, I have been gone,
I have been left to wrack and rot.

And yet I melt, and breathe, and live.
I am the secret you forgot.

I am the land, the sea, the hills,
The symbols of your fear and lack.

You tried to freeze the mountain's eyes,
But brother, see, you failed. I'm back.

Njord

Chapter One

'We interrupt this programme to bring you a severe weather warning. Flash storms are affecting many coastal regions again this morning. The authorities are advising people living in these areas to avoid going out unless they have to. Coastal roads still flooded from yesterday's downpour will remain closed until further notice.'

Mum switched the TV off and got up to put the kettle on. 'These storms are getting ridiculous,' she said. 'It's the middle of summer! We should be outside sunbathing, not huddled inside or dashing about under raincoats and umbrellas.'

Mum's best friend Millie nodded at the torn, inside-out brolly standing upside down in the bin. 'Third one I've been through in a week,' she said. 'I wouldn't mind so much if it was just the rain. It's the howling wind I don't like. It's been giving me bad dreams. And the waves crashing over the pier don't exactly help create a calm space for my Meditation and Visualisation group.'

'Meditation and Visualisation' was Millie's new class that she ran from *King*, the boat she lived on near us in Brightport harbour. *King* was our old boat, but we'd moved to a new one when my mum and dad were reunited. Mum's human and Dad's a merman and our boat, *Fortuna*, has been specially adapted so that you can live above and below water on it. I'm a semi-mer – human on land, mermaid in the water – which means I get to live both above *and* under water.

Millie was on week three of her Meditation and Visualisation group. She'd set it up after she'd had what she called 'an enlightened moment of synchronicity'.

'Enlightened moments of synchronicity' are the kinds of things Millie has a lot of. She doesn't worry too much that no one knows what such things actually mean.

'I don't see what the fuss is about,' I said. 'The

storms only last half an hour and the rest of the time the weather's been beautiful.' I glanced out of the window. 'Look, it's clearing up already.'

Mum and Millie exchanged a look.

'What?' I asked.

Mum reached for a couple of mugs and put a tea bag in one of them. 'Well, I'm not surprised *you* can look on the bright side,' she said, a hint of a smile twitching the corners of her mouth.

'What d'you mean?'

'She means it's funny how everything looks rosier to those of us who have got a *boyfriend*,' Millie said. Then she cackled with laughter and got up from the sofa. 'Only teasing, lovey, don't worry,' she went on, squeezing my cheek as she passed me. 'Earl Grey for me, Mary P,' she added, joining Mum in the kitchen.

'Whatever,' I said, turning away from them both, so they couldn't see the flames creeping up my cheeks – or the smile that I was finding it hard to keep off my face.

But they were right. I was finding it hard to look on the downside of *anything* at the moment. So what if it rained a bit? Who cared? As far as I was concerned, my world was full of sunshine.

And yes, it *was* because of Aaron. My boyfriend.

I still felt a bit weird calling him that, and I hadn't actually used the word out loud yet – especially to him! But I said it in my head – a lot. And I liked it.

Rap rappity rappity rap! A tap at the door broke me from my thoughts. I recognised the knock, and right on cue, my cheeks burned again.

Mum reached the door just ahead of me. 'Hello, Aaron,' she said with a big smile. 'We were just talking about you.'

Aaron glanced past Mum to catch my eye. 'Were you?' he asked shyly.

I squeezed past Mum. 'See you later,' I said as I kissed her cheek.

'Be careful out there,' she warned.

'It's fine. Look – the storm's finished already. Told you it wouldn't last long.' I headed down the jetty with Aaron.

'Have fun with your boyfriend!' Millie trilled from inside the boat.

I stole a glance at Aaron. 'Sorry about them,' I mumbled.

He smiled. 'I don't mind,' he said, 'if you don't.'

I looked down, too embarrassed to meet his eyes. 'No, I suppose I don't mind either,' I said to the wooden slats of the jetty.

Aaron reached out a hand without saying anything else, and I slipped my hand into his as we walked. As I did, I felt my whole body tingle and heat up. I'd never felt anything like the way I felt when Aaron held my hand. It was as if someone was tickling all my nerve endings at the same time. It made me want to jump up and down and burst out laughing.

We'd only met this year. Aaron used to live with his mum in a castle out at sea, but they'd recently moved to Brightport with us. We'd put on an amazing concert recently, and ever since that night – when he'd kissed me – I'd felt this way.

I didn't tell him, of course. The only person I'd said anything to was my best friend, Shona.

'You're in LOVE!' she'd squealed delightedly when I'd told her. Shona is the most traditional, soppy mermaid in the entire world, and loves nothing more than a good romance.

'Don't be ridiculous!' I'd said at the time. 'I'm too young to be in love. I don't even know what it means.' Like her, I was nearly thirteen – *way* too young to start thinking about things like love.

But I did find myself wondering about the word. And I *was* aware that there was nothing I liked more than being with Aaron. I was also aware that lately this had meant I hadn't seen as much of Shona as usual. And I had the feeling it was becoming a sore point.

I wasn't sure if she was bored of being the odd one out, or fed up with me talking about him, or maybe even a tiny bit jealous. Either way, she'd stopped asking me about Aaron. And whenever I tried to talk about him, she'd changed the subject or swum off to do something else.

I didn't really blame her. I must have become quite boring, talking about Aaron all the time. And to be honest, I missed hanging out with her. The only trouble was, I always wanted to hang out with Aaron *more*.

'What do you want to do?' Aaron asked now, as we walked up the jetty.

What I really wanted to do was go to the Rushton's fairground and take a ride on the ghost train so we could sit really close and hold hands in the dark. We'd been on it the other night, and even though it was the tamest ride in the world, I'd pretended to be scared so that Aaron would put his arm round me. It felt so nice I didn't want the ride to end. Unfortunately it did though, and since then I hadn't managed to find another excuse to snuggle up close to him.

But I hadn't seen Shona since the beginning of the week, and it was Friday now.

'Shall we go to Shiprock?' I suggested. Shiprock was the merfolk town under the sea where Shona lived.

'Sure!' Aaron agreed, and we walked down the beach to the water's edge.

Aaron waded into the water. I looked around nervously.

'It's fine,' he said. 'Come on.' Then he turned away and ran, splashing and jumping, into the water.

I still hadn't got used to the fact that we didn't have to hide what we were any more. It was only last year that I'd discovered I became a mermaid when I went in water – and for most of the time since then, it had been a secret. Neptune, who ruled the seas, used to be really strict about these things. For years and years, he'd kept the human and mer worlds apart and used a memory drug to make humans forget if they ever saw a mermaid. He even had laws that said humans and merpeople couldn't mix. My dad had been sent to prison because he'd married my mum!

But everything had changed recently. Neptune had decreed that humans and merpeople *had* to get on together. And he'd got rid of the memory drug – at least in Brightport – so everyone knew about merpeople and we no longer had any reason to hide.

Even so, it still felt weird to go into the water without panicking about what would happen if someone saw my tail.

'What are you waiting for?' Aaron called to me. Then he ducked under and flicked his tail above the waves. As he dived down, his tail shone like silver in the bright sunlight that was beaming down on us now that the morning's storm was over.

Aaron was a semi-mer like me, and his ease in the water reminded me how much I loved it, too. I shrugged off my worries and ran into the sea to join him.

Within seconds, I felt my body begin to change. First, the familiar tingle in my toes; then my legs went numb and joined together; finally, my legs disappeared altogether, my clothes melted away, and in their place my tail formed. I swished it around, stretching it out and spinning in the water to join Aaron.

We swam along side by side, and I smiled to myself and wondered if I had ever felt so happy in my whole life.

Shona's mum hovered in the door of their home in Shiprock Caves, and smiled apologetically. 'Sorry, Emily, Shona went out earlier with some of her school friends.'

'No worries,' I said. 'We'll find her.'

She went inside and Aaron and I swam back down the tunnel and out to the open sea. A line of silver fish followed us, swimming just below me and tickling my tummy as I swam.

'Now what?' Aaron asked.

I had a tiny pang of jealousy at the thought of Shona playing out with other friends – till I remembered I had no right to feel jealous. *I* was the one who kept abandoning *her* to be with Aaron. I could hardly complain if she chose to hang out with some of her friends from Shiprock. Real friends who didn't drop her when they got a boyfriend.

Then I had an idea. 'I know where she might be.'

The water grew colder as we made our way out to sea. Fish glanced furtively at us as we passed.

'Look,' Aaron said, laughing, as two fish swam towards us. One was fat and yellow with a purple blotch all over its face. It looked like a grand lady who'd smudged her lipstick. The other one had black and white stripes the length of its long body. It swam elegantly beside her, like an obedient butler.

We swam through a couple of arches in the rocks, going lower and lower till we came to a huge rug of brown seaweed flapping lazily in the tide.

'What's this place?' Aaron asked as we swam across the seaweed to a sandy patch covered in fishing nets, old bicycles and oil drums.

'It's our playground,' I said, swimming through a large tube and indicating for him to follow me.

We swam to the end of the tube and looked round; Shona wasn't there. Half of me was disappointed – but the other half felt relieved. At least she hadn't shared our special playground with all her other friends. Plus it meant I was free to carry on being alone with Aaron.

'Hey, look at this,' he called, swimming across to a black sheet at the far end of the playground. I hadn't seen it before.

I swam over to join him. 'What is it?'

'Looks like a sail to me.'

'A black sail?'

Aaron grinned. 'Must be from a pirate ship! Let's check it out.'

He lifted a corner for me, and my heart flipped like a silver fish flapping its fins. Maybe I *would* get to snuggle up to Aaron in the darkness after all!

The sand scattered below me as I swam down, and the sail wafted upwards, swishing with the tide. I swam onwards, only stopping when I heard Aaron call out.

I turned back. He wasn't there.

'Aaron?'

No reply.

'Aaron?' I called louder. 'You OK?'

Still nothing.

I started swimming back to the edge of the sail, but my tail snagged on something. A piece of seaweed? I twisted round to see what it was. As I turned, the seaweed pinched harder. My tail was completely stuck. A moment later, something grabbed me round my middle.

And then the world went black.

Chapter Two

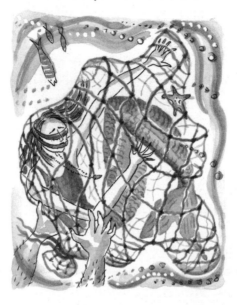

'Aaron, get off me,' I said, laughing. It was typical of him to play a joke like this. Pretend he wasn't following me, then sneak in and cover my eyes with his hands. Any second now, he'd say 'Guess who?' and it would be an easy guess.

But he wasn't saying anything.

'Come on, Aaron, I know it's you,' I said. I was still laughing. I reached up to his hands so I could pull them off.

And that was pretty much the moment I stopped laughing.

They weren't Aaron's hands.

The hands over my eyes were big, cold and clammy. 'Who – who is this?' I stammered.

Whoever it was spread one of their hands across both my eyes and clamped the other one across my mouth.

I couldn't speak. I could hardly breathe. My heart was beating so fast it felt like a motor boat's engine in overdrive. What was going on? How long would it take Aaron to realise that something wasn't right and come back for me?

I tried to bite the hand over my mouth but I couldn't even prise my lips wide enough apart to open my teeth. I tried to get my tail out of the seaweed – and realised that it wasn't seaweed – it was a net.

Then I heard a voice. Gruff. Muffled. Urgent.

'Tie her tail up,' the voice said. 'Slippery as an eel, this one.'

My tail felt as if it was being bent double as they bound it up. I felt hands wrap a thick band of reeds over my eyes and my mouth – and it was done. I was blind, dumb and trapped inside a net.

'Right, let's get out of here,' the gruff voice said. 'Now!'

I had no idea where I was being taken. All I knew was that the journey seemed to go on for ever, and that the sea felt as cold as the hands that gripped and carried and bustled me all the way there.

'Now what?' a voice said, some time later. It wasn't the gruff voice. It was a different one. Higher pitched. Smoother. Kinder? No, that was just wishful thinking.

'We do exactly what we've been told,' Gruff Voice answered. 'Keep her here and stay with her until we're given further instructions. The others should be here any minute.'

Others?

'Right.'

'You hold her, I'll sort out the locks.'

'Got it.'

As one set of hands released me, the others clutched tighter, squeezing me so hard I thought they'd crush me into sand.

Moments later, Gruff Voice was back. 'Right, we're locked in. Let's get her out of there.'

'Get her out?'

'She can't go anywhere, and we were told not to be too rough with her. We can't have the boss turn up and find her blindfolded and trussed up in a fishing net, can we now?'

'You're right. You sure the door is secure?'

'It's locked as tight as a shark's jaws. Come on, let's get her out of that net.'

I squirmed and struggled and fought as they undid the net and removed the reeds round my mouth and eyes. The second my mouth was free, I found my voice.

'AAARRRRRGGHGGGGGHHHHHLET MEGOYOUMONSTERRRRRRS!' I yelled

One of them clamped a hand over my mouth. I bit into his finger.

'Lumbering lobsters!' he yelped, leaping away from me. As he did, I looked him up and down. The gruff voice belonged to an even gruffer-looking merman. He was huge – at least seven foot from his head to the end of his long, sharp, dusty grey tail. He had greasy black hair tied back in a ponytail, grey eyes staring into mine, and what looked like an elaborate collection of Iron Age tools dangling from his ears, eyelids, chin and upper lip.

I wasn't sure I wanted to get on the wrong side of him.

'You can scream all you like,' he snarled, 'but no one will hear you. We're a long way down, and there's no one else around for miles.'

I listened for any response to my scream. There wasn't one – unless you counted the gentle sway of multicoloured sea bushes, or the shoal of a hundred tiny silver fish that darted towards me and then flicked away again, flashing like a knife in sunlight.

'Where are we?'

He didn't reply.

I cast a quick glance at the other merman: skinnier, younger, only about half the amount of piercings and maybe a foot shorter, but looking at me with the same expression. I wasn't exactly sure what the expression was. Hatred? Menace? Anger?

No. It wasn't any of those. Or if it was, it was mixed with something else. If they hadn't just grabbed me in a park and locked me in an underwater cell in the middle of the ocean, I'd have said they looked nervous – as though they weren't quite sure how to handle me. No, it couldn't be that. But what was it?

'What do you want with me?' I asked.

Gruff Voice ignored me as he rubbed his finger where I'd bitten it.

'I'm sorry about that,' I said.

Wait! These guys kidnap me in a net, blindfold me, gag me and drag me to a hidden cave, and I apologise to *them*? 'What do you want with me?' I repeated, more firmly. 'Why am I here? Who are you?'

Skinny Merman opened his mouth to answer me, but Gruff Voice held up a hand. The one I hadn't bitten. 'No answers,' he said.

'But, Orta—' the other merman began.

Gruff Voice – Orta – shook his head. 'But nothing, Kai. We have our instructions. No conversation, no explanation, no nothing. Got it?'

Kai nodded. 'Got it,' he mumbled.

They both fell silent after that. For the first time, I

looked around the cave and realised how big it was – and how grand. The roof seemed to glow with a hazy fluorescent light in between stones carved into intricate shapes all along the rocky ceiling.

I swam round the walls, feeling and examining them as I moved. They were filled with crystals. Natural sea crystals or some kind of exotic jewels, I couldn't tell. All I knew was that I hadn't been locked away in a prison cell. I'd seen an underwater prison cell when I'd rescued my dad – and it was nothing like this!

An occasional lone fish swam past, black and sleek, skittering quickly from one side to the other like a businessman on his way to a meeting. A long silver eel slithered by, slicing in front of me like a sword.

I swam towards the entrance: an enormous solid oak door with metal bars across it. It was bolted and fastened with the biggest padlock I'd ever seen.

That was when I heard something on the other side. Scuffling and shuffling outside the cave! What was it? A huge shoal of fish? The tide hitting against the door? Or was there a chance it was someone who could help me get out of here?

I banged on the door as hard as I could. Which wasn't actually very hard. I don't know if you've ever tried it, but it turns out that bashing your fists against a solid oak door half a mile down in the ocean is fairly pointless. All I managed to do was bruise my hands and make a soft thudding sound.

'HELP!' I yelled instead. 'I'M BEING HELD PRISONER! SAVE ME!'

The two mermen were by my side in seconds. 'I wouldn't waste your time,' Orta said.

'It'll just be some sort of big fish,' Kai added. 'A shark or something. Out here in the middle of the ocean, we get all sorts.'

That made me feel *so* much better.

'No it won't, you stupid seaworm!' Orta snapped, reaching for his key. 'It'll be the others. Get out of my way.'

A moment later, he'd opened the door, and a couple more mermen came in holding a package between them. A wriggling package trussed up in a net. For a second, I wondered what they'd brought us. And then the package spoke.

'Gtmtofhrrrrrr!' it said.

Wait! It was . . . It was . . .

Aaron!

'Get him out of that thing!' I yelled, angrier than ever. 'Let him out now!'

'Hold your halibut, we're *getting* him out!' Orta snapped. He pulled a long knife from a belt at the top of his tail, and with a couple of swift movements, the net was open.

Kai pulled off Aaron's blindfold and gag. Aaron blinked and gasped as he adjusted to his surroundings. As soon as he saw me, he swam to me and wrapped me in his arms.

'Emily,' he breathed. 'I didn't know what had happened to you. I was right behind you, and the next thing I knew, they . . .' He lowered his voice as he looked at the mermen who had brought him in, '. . . these pieces of sea vermin grabbed me.'

'Are you OK?' I asked.

He nodded. 'What about you? Did they hurt you? If they did, I'll—'

'I'm fine,' I said. 'At least, I am now,' I added, with as much of a smile as I could manage, given the circumstances.

Aaron smiled back, and pulled me closer. As long as I was with him, things didn't seem quite so bad.

'Delightful and touching as this little love scene is,' Orta said, breaking into my thoughts, 'we've got a job to do.' He looked at the mermen who had brought Aaron in. 'You can leave them both with us,' he said. 'We can manage.'

'You sure?'

'Sure as sharks.' He swam back to the door behind the two mermen. As he pulled the key from round his neck again, Aaron glanced at me and raised an eyebrow.

I knew what he was thinking. I was thinking the same. *This could be our chance to escape!* Without saying a word, we edged closer to the door while the mermen talked.

Orta put his key in the padlock. Turned it. Opened the door.

'*Now!*' Aaron hissed in my ear and I made a dash for the door.

'I don't think so!' Kai grabbed hold of my tail, gripping so hard I thought he'd break my scales off. Half a minute later, I was back inside the room, the door shut fast behind me.

Orta clicked the padlock into place and put the key back round his neck. He nudged a thumb at Kai. 'Just because he *looks* stupid doesn't mean he actually *is* stupid,' he said.

'Yeah,' Kai agreed. Then he scratched his head and looked at Orta. 'Oi!' he added, realising what Orta had said.

Orta brushed him off with a dismissive wave. 'You just need to be patient,' he said to us. 'I'm sure you won't be here much longer – one way or another.' He emphasised the 'one way or another' with a menacing laugh.

I swam back over to Aaron. He was examining the lights and crystals in the walls.

'Look at these,' he said. 'They're amazing.'

'Almost like jewels,' I said, shuffling closer.

Aaron shuffled closer to me, too. 'We'll be OK,

you know,' he said. 'We'll think of something.'

The strange thing was, when he smiled at me like he was doing, I couldn't help believing him.

'You're right,' I said. 'I think everything's going to be—'

Except I didn't get to finish my sentence. It was washed away by a wave that swooshed through the cave so suddenly and so fiercely it swept all four of us up to the ceiling and then hurled us against the opposite wall.

Orta was first to recover. He pulled himself up, brushed a hand down his tail and gave Kai a thump in the chest. 'Look sharp,' he said. 'Boss is coming.'

I shuddered to think what their boss was going to be like. These two were bad enough. How much worse would *he* be?

I didn't have long to wonder.

Three heavy bangs on the door, and Orta practically flew across the cave to open it. He unlocked the padlock, swung the bolt across and swam backwards, his head bowed low as he held the door open.

And then, pulled by a dozen dolphins, and riding a golden chariot that shone so brightly it lit the caves up like a firework display, in came their boss.

Neptune!

'You?' I gasped. 'But—'

With the briefest glance at Aaron and me,

Neptune turned to the mermen. 'Good work,' he said sombrely. 'You are relieved.'

Bowing low, Orta and Kai swam out of the cave without a backwards glance at either of us. Neptune raised his trident, and a dolphin at the back of the chariot flicked its tail to shut the door behind them.

'Right then,' he said gravely, turning to face us. 'Let's get down to business.'

Chapter Three

own to business? What did *that* mean? I was fairly certain I hadn't signed up to do any business with Neptune. It wasn't exactly the kind of thing you forgot. And it wasn't the kind of thing you volunteered for in a hurry, either.

In case you've never come across Neptune, he's the king of all the oceans. He used to rule with an iron rod – or rather, an iron trident. That's his special staff that he uses to do things like create storms or put curses on people.

But he'd softened recently. I'd thought he was happy and that everything was fine.

I was clearly wrong.

'You're probably wondering why I have brought you down here,' Neptune said in a low, deep voice that echoed and rumbled throughout the cave.

Er . . . yes!

'I shall tell you.' And then he fell silent.

He looked cross. And even though I'd seen Neptune look cross more times than I cared to remember, there was something different about this kind of cross. He didn't look cross with us. He looked cross with *himself*.

He suddenly lifted his trident in the air and turned to his dolphins. With a flick of the trident, he bellowed, 'Leave us! Return when I call you!'

The dolphins flipped and turned in a swift, instant movement. One of them flicked open the door and they dived through it, flipped it closed behind them, and left the three of us alone in the cave. Neptune beckoned us to come closer.

Aaron and I shuffled awkwardly towards him.

'I have a job for you,' he said. 'A . . . well, a kind of mission.'

'A mission?' Aaron asked. 'What sort of mission?'

'I can't tell you too much at this stage,' Neptune replied gravely. 'But I can tell you this – it is extremely important, extremely secret . . . and extremely dangerous.'

Great. This was sounding better by the second.

'Why us?' Aaron asked.

Neptune looked down and examined his hands. 'Why not?' he mumbled.

'Why *not*?' I asked. I could think of *lots* of reasons why not!

Neptune shrugged and waved his trident in an overly nonchalant manner. 'Because you are semi-mers,' he said flippantly. 'I thought you would do.'

He wasn't convincing me. He was trying too hard to sound casual. He didn't go to the kind of lengths he'd gone to with us because we 'would do'.

'If you just need semi-mers, why not send someone like Mr Beeston?' Aaron asked.

Mr Beeston was half human, half merman, and already worked for Neptune. In fact, he'd spent most of my life spying on Mum and me and reporting back to Neptune on his findings. When I'd found out, I was furious. But lately, he'd changed. He'd apologised too, and things were different now – so I'd forgiven him. It didn't mean I'd ever trust him again, though.

'Mr Beeston's surely the obvious candidate for your sneaky secret missions,' I pointed out.

Neptune shook his head. 'Beeston is not to know about this mission,' he said. Then he scratched his beard and screwed up his eyes. 'Actually, now I think about it, perhaps it's not such a bad idea. Beeston *could* come in handy.'

'Great,' I said. 'Does that mean we can go now?'

'Go?'

'You just said – Mr Beeston can do it.'

Neptune's face darkened. 'Mr Beeston can *not* do this,' he said firmly. 'He cannot *know* about it, cannot know the full truth, anyway. What he can perhaps do is chaperone the pair of you. With limited knowledge of the full task.'

'Your Majesty, forgive me, but can I just check I've got this right?' I said, summoning up all my courage to stare into his face till he met my eyes. 'This mission is something so secret that even Mr Beeston, one of your closest advisors, isn't to know the full truth of it, and yet you're telling us we've been chosen simply because we're semi-mers?'

Neptune turned away.

'Sir . . . Your Majesty,' Aaron stumbled. 'Is there something you're not telling us?'

'All right,' Neptune said. 'I admit it. It's not just because you are semi-mers.'

He paused for so long that my tail started to itch and twitch with impatience. A black and gold spotted fish that looked like a leopard weaved between us. Neptune watched the fish swim away, then turned back to us. 'It's because I'm sending you to a place filled with secrets and magic,' he said. Which didn't sound so bad, actually, till he added, 'And fear.'

Secrets, magic *and fear* didn't sound quite so enticing.

'It's a dangerous combination,' Neptune went on, in case we hadn't figured that out for ourselves.

'So why us?' Aaron asked again.

'Because you will need all of my powers for this mission,' Neptune replied.

'All of your powers? But we haven't got them any more,' I said.

Aaron and I had found a pair of magical wedding rings that Neptune and his wife Aurora had given to each other. We'd discovered that when we held hands while wearing the rings, we gained Neptune's magical powers. Very cool once we'd figured out what was going on – except Neptune didn't find it quite as much fun as we did, and he made us give our power back to him. That had been weeks ago.

Neptune fixed his eyes on me so hard I had to turn away. 'Yes, you have,' he said.

I opened my mouth to argue, but he went on. 'A short while after you gave your power back to me, I noticed something. When I was near you, I could feel it. A vibration. A sense that you still had some of my power in your hands. I was baffled. How was it that you had it again? So I watched you.'

I bit back a response. So we were back to the old ways? Neptune sending people to spy on us?

'And?' Aaron asked.

'And I soon had my answer.' Neptune looked

26

from Aaron to me, and back again. 'You kissed, didn't you?'

'*What?*' Aaron exploded. 'How do you ... When ... What . . .' he blustered. His face had turned bright red.

'Well, then,' Neptune said. 'That explains everything.'

'What do you mean? *What* does it explain?' I asked.

'I was on a visit to Shiprock last week and I noticed you two in the distance.'

I remembered that day. We'd swum to Rainbow Rocks and played in the water around the rocks holding hands and talking and laughing all afternoon.

'When I saw you, I felt the feeling between you – the happiness, the joy. And I did something that I am now ashamed of.'

'What did you do?' I asked.

Neptune wouldn't meet our eyes. 'I sent a spike of anger to you,' he said to the floor, brushing something off the end of his tail.

'A spike of anger?' I said. 'What's that?'

'I was jealous.'

'Jealous? Of us?' Aaron stared at Neptune.

'You had something that I had lost,' Neptune said, finally meeting our eyes. 'And it upset me – just for a moment. So I made a tiny whirlpool and sent it spinning your way. It wouldn't have done you any harm. I just wanted to knock you off your happy little perch for a moment.'

I tried to remember the whirlpool – but I couldn't. I couldn't recall anything other than the happy feelings I'd had all afternoon.

'There was no whirlpool,' Aaron said.

'Exactly. It didn't *reach* you. You were so wrapped up in your happy little bubble that you didn't even notice it, spinning close to the rocks, but unable to get any nearer to you.'

'Unable?' I asked.

'Because you were holding hands,' Neptune explained. 'Somehow or other, you had regained the power to overcome my magic.'

'But how?'

Neptune cut me off with a wave of his hand. 'That's what I asked myself. At one point I thought you had tricked me. You can't imagine how angry I was when I thought that.'

Er, we probably could, actually. Neptune being angry was *very* easy to imagine.

'I thought about it and thought about it, and, finally, I realised how it must have happened.'

'When we kissed?' Aaron said. 'That's how we got our powers back?'

'Exactly!'

'But why?' I asked.

'When Aurora and I were married, we infused our wedding rings with magical powers. The ones you gained when you brought the rings back together.'

'But we gave the rings *and* the magic back to you,' I insisted.

'Hear me out!' Neptune barked, reminding us who he was, and why it wasn't generally wise to argue with him. 'At our wedding ceremony, we sealed the magic with a kiss. That kiss bound the magic firmly into the rings. The kiss was part of the magic. Powerful enough on its own to double the original powers.'

Aaron frowned. 'So when we kissed, it brought back *our* powers?'

'Precisely. I didn't know it would happen. But then I didn't know *any* of it would happen. The vows we made that day were for us and only us. They were never designed to be used by anyone else.'

'We didn't exactly do it on purpose,' I mumbled.

'No. You didn't – which is why you are not being punished.'

I looked round the cave, remembering the way I had arrived here. 'Really?' I asked.

'Yes, *really*!' Neptune snapped. 'In fact, it is quite the opposite. I realise that my method of bringing you here was perhaps not the best way of inspiring your loyalty and your trust.'

You think?

'But it guaranteed the one thing that I need above all else. Secrecy. No one is to know where you have gone, or why you have been brought here.'

I swallowed. I wasn't sure I wanted to hear any more. Not that I had a choice in the matter.

'I need you to do something for me,' he went on. 'It involves travelling a long distance. It involves risk, danger, and many unknown factors. The only thing about it that I can guarantee for sure is that if you do not do it . . .'

He stopped and shook his head.

'If we don't do it, what?' Aaron asked.

Neptune met Aaron's eyes. 'There is a threat ahead of us. It is coming closer,' he said. 'If you do not remove this threat, I don't think any of us will survive.'

'None of us?' Aaron asked in a shaky voice. 'Even you?'

'*Especially* me.'

'I . . . I don't understand,' I said.

Neptune leaned back against his chariot and curled his tail up beneath him. 'I can't tell you much, but I shall tell you what I know. You must understand something, though. You are the first and only ones I have told this to, and it must stay that way. Understand?'

Neptune was trusting *us* with a secret that no one else knew. Were we up to it? I flicked my tail and held myself straighter in the water. I glanced at Aaron and he nodded back at me.

'We understand,' we said in unison.

'Every morning for the last two weeks, I have woken drenched in sweat and writhing in the agony of terrors I can barely describe,' Neptune began. 'I cannot see the exact nature of the terrors, I can merely feel them.'

'You *feel* them?' I asked. 'You mean like someone's hurting you?'

'No one is there. No one is near. There is only myself,' Neptune replied. 'And my mind.'

'Your mind? You mean you're *imagining* the terrors?' Aaron asked.

Neptune's eyes darkened. For a moment he looked more like his usual self. '*Imagining?*' he said angrily. 'You think the king of all the oceans IMAGINES terrors?'

Aaron gulped. 'N-no, Your Majesty,' Aaron stammered. 'I'm sorry. I thought you said—'

Neptune ignored him and carried on. 'Every night in my sleep, I have been plagued by terrors, by images, feelings,' he said, almost to himself. 'It happens just before the dawn breaks, and appears as the most terrifying series of images – scenes which have aroused such emotion in me I've been unable to hide it. You must have noticed.'

'Noticed? We haven't seen you,' Aaron said.

'What happens when I'm angry or upset?' Neptune asked impatiently.

And then I got it! The weather. It was Neptune! His moods could create violent storms. The small, devastating storms we'd been having in the mornings were all because of Neptune's nightmares!

'You made the storms!'

He nodded. 'I can't help it. And they will get worse if this isn't stopped.'

'And that's why it's such a threat?' I asked.

'No. That is bad enough, for sure. But the threat is what I'm *seeing* in the dreams. I don't know what it is, but there's something out there, something that . . .' His voice trailed off.

'Something that scares you,' I said. He turned away and nodded.

'I don't understand,' Aaron said. 'You're *Neptune*! How can you be so scared of dreams?'

Neptune turned his cold, hard eyes on him. 'Because they aren't just dreams,' he said.

'What do you mean? If they aren't dreams, what are they?'

Neptune flicked his tail and bent down so he was almost at eye level with us. He was so close I could see the white hairs of his moustache as they crept up his nostrils, and smell the herring he'd had for his lunch.

And then, in a quivering voice that I would never normally have associated with Neptune, he said, 'They are memories.'

Chapter Four

*A*aron and I stared at Neptune.

'Memories?' I asked.

Neptune nodded. 'I think so. Earlier this year, I undid the memory drug on this whole area, remember?'

Of course we remembered. We'd been part of why he'd done it! Ever since then, people had recalled all sorts of mermaid memories that they'd forgotten about for years.

'Even *I* was not immune,' Neptune went on. 'It seems that there are now memories knocking on the door of my mind. There is something there, something that somebody has tried to hide from me, but it is returning – and it is wrapped in a dark threat.' He glared at both of us. 'Your job is to find the threat and remove it – and find the culprit who tried to steal my memories in the first place.'

Oh, was that *all*?

'Your Majesty, forgive me for asking, but if this is so important and so dangerous, why aren't you doing it yourself?' Aaron asked.

'There is great danger ahead,' Neptune said. 'To us all – and to the seas and the land. From my dreams – from my memories – I have a great sense that my presence on this mission would be a terrible mistake, and I cannot afford to make a mistake or to do the wrong thing. There is too much at stake.'

He stopped speaking, but he wouldn't look at us.

'You're scared!' I said.

Neptune raised his chin. He paused for a long time. Then, finally, he lowered his head and uttered one quiet word. 'Yes.'

That small word was almost more frightening than anything else he'd said. The fact that there was something out there that scared *Neptune* meant that it should scare us all.

I swallowed hard, and tried to stop my tail from shaking.

'I shall not say any more until I have your word,' Neptune said.

'Our word about what?' asked Aaron.

'Two things. One, that you are in this with me. And two, that everything you have heard today and anything you hear from me in the coming days will be between us, and only us.'

He looked from me to Aaron, inviting us and challenging us at the same time. I didn't look at Aaron. I didn't need to. By now, I knew how his mind worked. It worked the same way mine did – was driven by the same things: excitement, danger, adventure. Even though it made me quake with so many nerves my scales were standing on end, I knew what my answer would be – and I knew Aaron's would be the same. I'd have to think of a way to get Mum and Dad to agree – but we'd deal with that when the time came.

Without even a glance in each other's direction, Aaron and I replied in unison.

'We're in.'

It all happened really quickly after that.

Neptune flicked his trident and called out to his dolphins. A moment later, they returned to the cave.

'Come,' he said, beckoning us to join him in his chariot.

The dolphins sped us out of the cave, through all the winding tunnels we'd been brought down blindfolded earlier, and up into an area so grand it couldn't have been mistaken for anything other than one of Neptune's palaces. Giant pillars that seemed to be made of solid gold stood in each corner. Jewels filled the rocky ceiling. Light bounced around, dazzling my eyes as much as the chariot ride had dazzled my mind.

Even the fish that weaved around us seemed to swim with an air of importance. A lion fish that looked as if it had put on its grandest outfit glided across the atrium looking as regal as a duchess. Jet black fish with serious faces and sharp beady eyes swam by without glancing our way, aloof and superior.

We wound our way through the grand entrance hall to an enormous pair of doors. With a flick of his trident, Neptune called 'OPEN!' and the doors drew apart.

A moment later, we were back out in the open sea. The water was dark and murky after Neptune's palace, and I rubbed my eyes. Neptune indicated for us to leave the chariot. We slid over the side and flicked our tails, treading water as he explained where we were and how to find our way home.

Then he said, 'Come to the palace gates at six o' clock tomorrow morning.'

Six o' clock in the *morning*?

'You must be there when I awake. I need to tell you my dreams as soon as my eyes open. I don't want you to miss anything. Do you understand me?'

We nodded.

'Good. Then I shall see you in the morning.'

'What will we tell our parents?' I asked.

Neptune turned his dark eyes on me. 'You'll think of something.'

Aaron cleared his throat. 'How will we—'

'The dolphins will bring you,' Neptune said impatiently. 'Come to this point here, and they will meet you – at six precisely. The dolphins know where to find me. They will bring you to my side. I wake at half past six. You will be there. No one else must know where you are, or why you are there. I repeat – no one. We are clear on this?'

'Yes, Your Majesty,' I said.

'Totally clear,' Aaron added.

'Very well,' Neptune said, turning away from us and flicking his trident to give the dolphins their orders. 'Until tomorrow.'

A second later, we were dismissed and Neptune, the dolphins and the chariot were gone.

Aaron and I hovered in the murky water for a little while without speaking. It was hard to know what to say.

Below us, thick green tubes of seaweed brushed against dusty pink coral as it swayed in the current. Fish of all sorts of shapes and sizes swam towards us, around us, away from us, taking a peek before deciding we weren't all that interesting and darting away again.

We started swimming in the direction Neptune had told us. We swam in silence most of the way. I was busy going over everything that had happened and trying to make some sort of sense of it all. I guessed Aaron was doing the same.

Finally, when we were still quite a way from Brightport, Aaron slowed down and turned to me.

'You OK?' he asked.

'I don't know,' I replied honestly. 'You?'

Aaron tried a wonky smile. 'I think so,' he said. 'I'm glad we've got each other.'

I smiled back. 'Me too.'

'What are we going to say to our families?' I asked.

'We could say we're meeting up to swim to Rainbow Rocks and watch the sunrise together?'

'Good idea. Save them asking too many questions.'

But as we approached Brightport, I couldn't stop my mind from asking its own questions. What if we couldn't fulfil Neptune's mission? What if we got hurt – or worse?

'Hey, slowcoach. Race you to Brightport pier!' Aaron called from ahead of me, breaking into my thoughts before they spiralled out of control.

'You're on!' I pushed the questions to the back of my mind, flicked my tail as hard as I could and sped through the dark water.

The next morning, when my alarm clock went off at half past five, I leapt out of bed thinking there was a fire. Then I remembered – it was worse then a fire. It was a date with Neptune and his nightmares.

Aaron was outside the boat as soon as I closed the door behind me. 'Ready?' he asked.

I laughed drily. That was about the best I could manage as a reply.

We set off for the open ocean.

About half an hour later, we reached the palace. The dolphins were waiting for us outside the doors, just as Neptune had said they would be. We climbed aboard the chariot and they took us inside.

Twenty twists and turns and fifty chandeliers

later, we arrived at an arched door with a golden doorknob and a sparkling trident on the front, built into a rocky wall. The dolphins pulled to a halt.

'I guess this is our stop,' I said.

We clambered down from the chariot and the dolphins turned and swam away. We were alone, outside Neptune's room.

Finally, Aaron decided to be the brave one. Gently turning the knob, he pushed against the door. It opened. We swam inside.

It was the biggest room I had ever seen, anywhere. It was perhaps the size of a big stage in a theatre – and about as dramatic. The room was full of weird and wonderful furniture: a chaise longue in the shape of a giant lobster, an enormous cushion that looked like purple silk but could just as easily have been a giant eel wrapped round and round itself, coral-covered rocks lighting up the floor below our tails, a curtain of falling water across the centre of the chamber.

We swam across the room looking for Neptune. We could hear him; the snores sent vibrations through the whole place so hard it made my teeth rattle. They were coming from the other side of the waterfall curtain. We swam towards it, pushed through it – and stopped.

On the other side, we saw Neptune. At least, we saw bits of him. He was lying inside something that *could* have been a piece of furniture – the grandest, largest piece of them all, an amber bed, with Neptune on the inside, and eight pillars around him, twirling upwards and tailing into a spiral above him. The pillars began to move and twitch as we approached – which was when we realised they weren't pillars. They were—

'An octopus!' Aaron blurted out. 'Neptune sleeps on an *octopus*?'

I looked again, and just about managed to stop myself from turning and swimming straight out of there and never coming back. It looked so similar to something I'd seen before, and *never* wanted to see again. The kraken. Neptune's special pet. The one I'd woken early from its hundred-year sleep. The one that nearly destroyed a whole island, not to mention a cruise ship full of people – including my mum.

But Aaron was right. This wasn't the kraken. Its tentacles weren't filled with slime and goo and disgusting purple suckers. They looked, like everything else around here, as though they were filled with jewels. Triangles of light bounced off the suckers as they wafted with the movement of the water. No, this was just a harmless, innocent – *enormous* – octopus, which happened to serve the role of being Neptune's bed.

I had begun to think about the possibility of

relaxing a little when Neptune suddenly let out a roar.

'NOOOOOO! You will not!' he shouted. 'The water! Fetch the water! I'm cold. So cold. Quick, catch the water. Catch it! Before it's too late! Before it . . .'

What was he talking about?

A wave suddenly grabbed me, rolled me around like a snowball and hurled me across the room. The room was shaking. The walls vibrating. The chandeliers jangling. *What was happening?*

Another, more violent, wave picked me up and threw me again. This time I landed next to Aaron. He was holding onto a dagger-shaped stalactite on the ceiling. He held out his other hand. 'Take it!' he yelled. I scrabbled through the current and reached out. Missed. Tried again, but got caught in a whirling current that spun me round as if I was an old pair of jeans on a spin cycle.

Finally, I lunged against the tide and grabbed Aaron's hand. Instantly, the water calmed. The spin cycle stopped. The room quietened and stilled. A minute later, it was as if it had never happened. Was Neptune right about us still having his power? Had we stopped his storm with our hands? Or had the storm merely worked its way out and finished of its own accord? I didn't have long to think about it, as Neptune called us over.

We swam across the room to see the giant octopus

slowly unfurl itself as Neptune sat up inside it, his tail draped lazily in between two of the octopus's tentacles.

'You came,' he said simply.

'You ordered us to,' I pointed out.

Neptune half smiled. 'Quite. Well, then. On to business. Let me tell you about my dream.'

'Business' was basically listening to Neptune talk for an hour, and trying to pick out the bits that . . .

a) made any sense,
b) might help us figure out how to prepare for our mission, and
c) gave us some indication about the minor details, like, oh, you know, where we actually needed to go.

Unfortunately, there wasn't much of *any* of these. From the bits we'd overheard Neptune shouting in his sleep, and from what he told us when he woke up, this was what we *had* worked out so far . . .

Wherever we were going, it was cold, *really* cold.

There was something to do with water.

And possibly mountains.

And that was about it.

It was the same thing the next day: Neptune screaming out in his sleep, a brief but very violent storm, and an extremely limited amount of helpful information.

By the third morning, I was starting to feel exhausted from waking up so early every day. On top of which, it felt as if we weren't getting anywhere.

That afternoon, Aaron and I were hanging out on *Fortuna*, going over the things Neptune had told us and trying to find some way to piece it all together. It felt as though he'd given us a bag full of jigsaw pieces and told us to make a picture – except the pieces didn't fit together. They didn't even seem to be part of the same puzzle!

Mum was getting ready to go to her Pilates class when she burst into my bedroom, leggings on, sweatband round her head, tracksuit jacket round her waist. 'Emily, darling, would you be a love and nip round to Millie's for me? I've torn a hole in my gym socks and can't find the needle and thread anywhere. I'm sure she'll have some. I'd go myself but I have to stay and finish my book before tonight's book group.'

I didn't bother to make any comment on Mum's ridiculously packed social life – or equally ridiculous outfit.

'Course,' I said, and Aaron and I headed over to *King*, Millie's boat.

I climbed aboard and pushed the door open. 'Millie!'

No reply. We were about to leave when I heard something. She must have been down on the lower level. She'd had the boat adapted so that her boyfriend, Archie, could visit. He's one of Neptune's closest advisors, and a merman. The lower section of the boat had trapdoors like ours, so you could get to it from above or below.

I opened up the trapdoor and was about to shout down, when I saw who had made the sound. Archie.

'Oh,' I said.

He turned round. 'Oh, hi, Emily!' he said, with a big smile. It seemed false to me. Not that Archie doesn't smile much – just, well, he doesn't usually show *all* his teeth when he does. He looked like a dog flashing its fangs at an intruder.

'I was just, er, just leaving,' Archie said. 'Just popped over to see if Millie was here. I was going to surprise her. Take her on a date. You know, being spontaneous and that. But – well. She's not here, so, 'bye then. I'll tell her you called round.'

And before I had a chance to reply, he was gone. I stood there, holding the trapdoor open, staring down at the empty deck for a few moments, wondering if it was my imagination or if that had been a little weird.

'Is she there?' Aaron called from the door.

46

I went back to join him. 'Nope. Just Archie. He'd come to take Millie on a surprise date,' I said.

'Aww, they're so romantic, those two.'

Aaron was right. Archie probably wasn't being weird. He was always doing sweet things like that. All this scheming and secrecy with Neptune was making me paranoid.

'My mum will have some thread I'm sure. Let's go get it from mine,' Aaron said.

We left *King* and headed over to Aaron's house.

It was on the fourth morning that we finally had a breakthrough.

The storms hit us on the way to the palace. 'Are we late?' I asked, as we battled against the swell.

Aaron shook his head. 'He must be waking early.' We were spun round and washed against rocks all the way. By the time we arrived, we were both a bedraggled mess. The dolphins picked us up at the gates as usual, and sped to Neptune's quarters.

Neptune was reclining on the lobster-shaped chaise longue. He beckoned us into the room and we nervously swam towards him.

'Sorry we're late,' I began. 'We got caught in—'

'It doesn't matter,' Neptune said. 'You're here now.' He smoothed his beard and spoke quickly. 'My dreams were especially vivid this morning – such strong visions that I know without question these are memories. The places I visited – it was as though I were there. Look!'

He held out his hand. 'Touch it,' he said.

I felt his hand. It was like ice. 'Youch!' I said, pulling my hand away.

'You see. It's real!' Neptune exclaimed, his eyes wide and wild. 'It's coming for me! It's *in* me!'

By now, we'd become used to him talking in riddles, so we didn't interrupt.

Neptune leapt off his chaise longue and began to swim around us. He flicked his tail as he swam and a line of bubbles followed him in a wavy trail. 'I felt the ice. I saw it – saw where it had come from,' he said. 'There is a lake – it has something to do with the memories – a lake where you must meet your eyes and jump. And there is water – frozen at the top of a mountain. You must find this water. Only you can hold it. You must do that. You understand? And you must find the lake. Do this and you will also find the threat – and the traitor.'

He stopped swimming and, gripping his trident, stared into our eyes. 'Above all, I finally know the most important thing. I know where it is. I know where I am sending you.'

Aaron swallowed. 'Where?' he asked shakily.

Neptune lowered his voice and leaned in close. Almost in a whisper, he said, 'To the Land of the Midnight Sun.'

Chapter Five

*T*he Land of the Midnight Sun? Where on earth was that? We stared at Neptune open-mouthed, waiting for him to explain.

The only trouble was, he didn't.

'We haven't got long,' he went on hurriedly. 'You're leaving this weekend.'

'This weekend?' I gasped. 'As in, four days' time?'

'Well, technically, three days. You'll be off on Friday.'

'Friday,' I said, just to confirm I'd heard right. Three days to get our parents to agree to let us go off on a dangerous mission that we couldn't even tell them about. 'And we're going to the Land of the Midnight Sun,' I added. 'Which is?'

'Which is in the very far north of the planet,' Neptune said. 'A place where, for many weeks in the summer, the sun does not set.'

'At all?' Aaron asked.

'At all. It is constant daylight. Now, listen. I have told you about a mountain, and about a lake. They are linked. The lake is surrounded by the mountains. You must find this place. When you gaze into the lake, you will not be able to see the bottom – all you will see is the reflection of the mountains around it. But here is the thing – the reflection will not match the reality.'

'Huh?' I said.

'I can't explain better than that,' Neptune said. 'All I know is that what you will see around you is not exactly what you will see in the lake. You must find this lake. One of the mountains surrounding it is covered in a glacier that looks like a giant's tongue spreading down the mountain. This is where you will find my answers.'

I let out a breath. So basically we needed to find a place where what we saw wasn't really there, and then climb up a tongue into a giant's mouth. Excellent.

Neptune swam across the room and beckoned for us to follow. Batting away a brown and cream striped fish that looked as if it were dressed in pyjamas, he reached into a drawer with handles like cobras, and took out two shells. 'Take these,' he said, passing us one each.

I turned the shell over in my hands. It was shiny purple, with a spiral winding tightly round the top, opening up into a fatter shape in the middle, with a big gap that went into the centre of the shell. The kind of shell you'd hold to your ear so you could hear the ocean. Aaron's was silver. Neptune held a third one; it was gold.

'You will use these to communicate with me. They are not ordinary shells. They are shell *phones*. They are infused with my magic, and with them you can contact me – no matter where you are, no matter what time of day or night.'

'How do we use them?' I asked, turning my shell over in my hands.

'You say out loud the colour of the phone you want to speak to – purple, silver or gold – and that person's shell phone will light up. When they pick it up, speak into your shell. They will hear you. Are we clear?'

We nodded.

'I need you to keep me up to date with any important information.'

I opened my mouth to ask a question. He answered it before I had the chance.

'If you don't know whether something is

important or not, assume it is and contact me. Understand?'

'We understand,' we said together.

'Good. Now, take these as well.' He reached back into the drawer and pulled out two small bottles. He handed us one each.

'What are these?' I asked, studying my bottle. It looked like the kind of thing Millie kept her herbs and potions in – a tiny glass bottle with a cork in the top and a bright orange liquid inside that shimmered and glowed like smoke from a flare.

'The sea where you are going is far, far colder than anything you have swum in before,' Neptune said. 'Full merfolk can adapt to all waters, but you are semi-mers and do not have that power. The first time you enter the water, you must put this on your scales. It will protect you. Use the whole bottle and it will let you swim in these waters for a week. That should be plenty of time.'

Should be? What if it *wasn't*? What if the mission took longer than that? I didn't ask out loud. If Neptune thought a week was long enough for this mission, I didn't want to argue for us to take longer.

'Next,' Neptune said briskly, 'I will arrange a cover for you.'

'A cover?' I asked.

'No one is to know where you are going, or why.'

I considered pointing out that seeing as, strictly

speaking, *we* didn't actually know where we were going, he was pretty safe on this one.

'Mr Beeston will escort you,' Neptune went on. 'He will be told that this is a special secret task for me – but he will not be told about the nightmares, or the extent of the threat.'

'Why Mr Beeston?' I asked. 'Why not our parents?'

'Beeston can live on land and in the sea,' Neptune explained. 'Both may be needed. And for all his faults, he can be trusted.'

I swallowed any reply to *that*.

'I will arrange all the details and send Beeston to see you when it is done,' Neptune continued. 'Are we clear?'

Were we clear? I held back a nervous laugh.

'Listen,' Neptune said. 'This is all you need to know: there is a threat; it is big; it will come from the Land of the Midnight Sun; you are to stop it and find out who stole my memory. It's as simple as that.'

The nervous laugh I was holding back froze in my stomach as the extent of our task really began to sink in.

'I will always be grateful to you,' he added. 'When this is over, there will be rewards.'

'We understand,' Aaron said.

Finally finding my voice, I added, 'We'll do everything we can. We won't let you down.'

Neptune looked at us both and smiled. 'I know you won't,' he said. 'That is why I chose you.'

Neptune was true to his word in getting things organised.

The next morning, Aaron was over at my place. Aaron's mum and Millie were round, too. Millie was reading Mum's tarot while Aaron and I looked on and tried not to burst out laughing every time she said things like, 'The empress next to the four of cups – very auspicious,' in a deep, meaningful voice.

Dad turned up halfway through the reading, poking his face through the trapdoor in the floor and leaning his arms over the side as he blew a kiss to Mum.

'Shhhhh!' Millie hissed. 'I'm fully attuned and I don't want you disturbing the spiritual essence of the tarot.'

Which made me want to laugh even more.

Just as Millie was finishing the reading and had begun to shuffle her cards, there was a sharp rap on the door.

'Only me,' Mr Beeston called as he stepped onto the boat and looked around. 'Ah, good. I'm glad you're all here. I have some important news.'

'Sounds ominous,' Millie said.

'Not at all,' Mr Beeston said. 'In fact it's very exciting news.' He turned to Aaron and me, then looked back at the others and smiled his wonky smile. 'It concerns Emily and Aaron.'

'Uh-oh,' Dad said with a wink. 'What have they got up to now?'

Mr Beeston gave Dad one of his *I'm-very-important-and-I-know-a-lot-more-than-you* looks. 'What they have "got up to" is impressing Neptune so much with all their recent actions that he has decided to reward them,' he said.

'What kind of reward?' asked Mum.

Mr Beeston cleared his throat. 'He's sending them on a holiday.'

'A holiday? Oh, how wonderful!' Mum said, almost bouncing in her seat. 'Where are we going? When are we off?' She jumped off the sofa. 'Ooh, what do I need to pack?'

'Ah, well, that's the thing.' Mr Beeston reddened.

Mum stopped bouncing. 'What's the thing?'

'You . . . er . . . well, you don't need to pack anything, actually. At least, not for yourselves.'

Mum stared at him for a moment, and then brightened again. 'You mean Neptune is providing us with everything we need?'

'Neptune is not providing *you* with anything!' He fiddled with the bottom of his jacket as he added, 'I'm afraid you won't be going.'

Mum and Dad exchanged a glance. 'They're going *alone*?' Dad asked.

Mr Beeston flushed even deeper. 'No, not alone,' he said. 'They will, of course, have a chaperone to escort them. Neptune has thought carefully about this important decision, and has come to the conclusion that he must send one of his most highly trusted, elite, superior—'

'YOU?' Mum burst out. 'He's sending *you*?'

'Er, yes,' Mr Beeston said, suddenly noticing something very important to look at on the deck.

'Why not us?' Dad asked.

'He . . . er . . . well, I mean, apart from the fact that I have been a highly trusted member of his staff for many years, I suppose he—'

'He wanted someone with a tail *and* legs,' Aaron cut in.

'At least, that's what we would guess,' I added quickly, glaring at Aaron. We weren't meant to know anything about this yet!

'Yes, that's what I meant,' Aaron blustered. 'I mean, it makes sense, doesn't it?'

Mr Beeston gave us one of his funny sideways looks. Did he know we already knew about this? That we knew more than *he* did?

'The children are probably right,' he said. 'Neptune would have wanted a semi-mer to go with them. *And*, of course, someone he trusted. Someone of a high rank. We leave on Friday.'

Mum tried to look pleased for us, but failed. 'You will look after them, won't you?' she said eventually.

'Of course I shall look after them,' Mr Beeston said. 'That is precisely my job.'

Dad smiled at us. 'Well, I think it's great,' he said. 'I'm proud of you both.'

'Me too,' Aaron's mum added, coming over to give Aaron a hug.

It was only when Dad said, 'Hey, kids, you could look a bit happier about it, you know,' that I realised we were meant to be acting as though we really *had* just found out we were going on a wonderful, all-expenses-paid holiday.

'We were just in shock,' Aaron said woodenly. 'It's great news, isn't it, Em?'

'It's fantastic,' I said, pinning a smile on my face. 'Yay,' I added for good measure, trying very hard not to let anyone see how much I was shaking.

Just then, there was a noise from the lower deck. Dad looked down. 'It's Archie,' he said. 'Come on up,' he called to Archie. 'You're just in time to hear the news.'

Archie swam up and joined Dad leaning on the trapdoor. Millie went over and bent down to kiss him.

'What news is that?' Archie asked, smiling broadly at Millie. Honestly, those two were *so* loved up – they were worse than Mum and Dad!

'We're going on a holiday!' Aaron said, making a

bit more effort to sound as though he believed it were true, and didn't actually know that we were being sent to a place so scary and so dangerous that Neptune himself didn't want to go there.

'That's wonderful,' Archie said, still smiling. 'All of us?'

'No – just Emily and Aaron,' Millie trilled. 'It's Neptune's treat!'

Archie's smile faded instantly, like a dark cloud coming out of nowhere to cover the sun and make everything cold. 'Neptune's *what*? Neptune's sending them away? Where are they going?'

Mr Beeston took a step forward and cleared his throat in his *I-know-you-work-for-Neptune-but-I'm-clearly-the-most-important-person-here* kind of way. 'It is by way of a thank you, a reward as it were,' he said. 'Emily and Aaron have done some great things lately, and this is Neptune's way of showing his gratitude.'

Archie nodded slowly. 'I understand,' he said. 'In that case, I have to go to see Neptune now. They will need escorting. I must insist I go with them.'

'Oh, darling, you're so lovely,' Millie said, gently stroking his cheek. 'You'd do anything to help Neptune, wouldn't you?'

'Of course I would,' Archie said.

'Ah, well, actually, it's all sorted,' Mr Beeston said. 'I have already been asked to escort them. So, on this occasion, you won't be needed.'

Archie's face paled. He stared at Mr Beeston, no doubt angry at being shown up in front of us all. 'I have to go,' he said eventually. 'I'll see you later.' And with that, he flicked his tail, dived back down to the lower deck and swam away.

'Huh!' Millie said. 'He didn't even kiss me goodbye!'

'Well, at least he seemed pleased for us,' I said sarcastically. I mean, what exactly was his problem?

'He's probably just jealous that he wasn't Neptune's first choice as chaperone,' Mr Beeston said, a little smugly.

'Hey, did he mention that we popped over to see you on Monday, by the way, about five o' clock?' I asked Millie.

'No. Are you sure?' Millie asked.

'Positive,' Aaron replied. 'Archie was there. He said he'd come over to take you out on a surprise date.'

Millie smiled indulgently. 'How sweet, but you must have the wrong day. Archie knows full well that I have my Aura Reading class then. I wouldn't cancel it for anything – not even a date with him!'

We hadn't got the wrong day, but I didn't say anything. If Millie wanted to believe Archie was the most romantic being on the planet, let her. I wasn't quite so sure *what* he was. Right now, he seemed to be turning into someone who just acted strangely. Or maybe I was letting everything get to me too much.

I suddenly felt the need to escape. 'I'm going out,' I said.

'But you can't; you've got to pack for your holiday!' Mum exclaimed.

'Are you all right, little 'un?' Dad asked.

'Shall I come with you?' Aaron added.

'I'm fine. I can pack later. I just need to be on my own for a bit,' I said. I didn't want to be with any of them right now.

It was only once I'd left the boat that I knew exactly where I needed to go, and who I needed to see. And I couldn't get there fast enough.

'Emily!' Shona opened her front door and swam out to meet me. She took hold of my arm. 'Come on in; Mum and I are making crab cakes.'

'Can you come out instead?' I asked.

'What's wrong? Are you OK?'

'I just want to hang out on our own.'

Shona smiled. 'Swishy – it's been ages! I'll tell Mum I'm going out.' She disappeared inside.

I felt guilty at that. I knew she meant that I was always with Aaron nowadays.

'Mum says I've got to be back in an hour,' Shona

said, swimming back and shutting their big porthole door behind her. 'Where d'you want to go?'

'Rainbow Rocks?' That was where I'd first met Shona, and who knew — maybe this would be the last time I'd ever see her, if it all went wrong.

We swam to the biggest of the rocks and pulled ourselves to the water's edge. Shona perched on the edge of the rock, her tail flapping in the water. I lay on my tummy at the sea's edge, flicking my tail in the waves behind me.

'Shona, I've got something important to tell you,' I said.

Shona's tail stopped flapping. 'What is it?' she asked. 'Is it you and Aaron? Have you fallen out?'

'What? No! Of course we haven't!'

'Oh, good,' Shona said, although I'm sure I saw a tiny flicker of disappointment in her eyes. 'What then?'

'I . . . I've got to go away,' I began.

'Away where? For how long? When?' Shona fired questions at me.

'I don't know for how long,' I said. 'I'm leaving the day after tomorrow.'

'How come you haven't told me this till now?' She looked hurt. Then her face seemed to close up. 'Are you going with Aaron?'

How was I meant to explain? I wasn't allowed to tell anyone anything, but I really wanted to give her something. I didn't want her to think I was just going off with Aaron on a big adventure that she was excluded from.

Then I realised what I could give her. I reached into my tail pocket and pulled out something that I always carried with me: my friendship pebble. Shona and I had given each other these ages ago as a symbol of our friendship – and of the fact that we would always be there for each other, no matter what.

'I want you to have this,' I said.

'But it's yours!' Shona said. 'If I take it, what will you have?' Then her eyes danced with an idea. She reached into her own tail pocket and pulled out her identical pebble. 'Let's swap them! That way, we both have something really special of each other's.'

'Kind of like saying we're not really apart?'

'Exactly!'

We swapped pebbles, and Shona looked a bit happier. But it still wasn't enough. I wanted to give her more. Then I had a thought. I had my shell from Neptune on me. What if I gave it to Shona? We'd still have Aaron's so we could talk to Neptune, but it would mean I could keep in touch with Shona while we were away, too. And it would *really* show her how important she was to me.

Before I could talk myself out of it, I pulled the shell out of my pocket. 'Shona, take this,' I said.

She looked at the shell. 'What is it?'

I took a breath. How much could I tell her? 'Neptune has organised this trip,' I said. 'He's told everyone it's a holiday, but . . .' I stopped. 'Look, *promise* you won't tell anyone.'

'Of course I won't. I thought you knew you could trust me.'

'I do. That's why I'm telling you.' I glanced round nervously and lowered my voice. 'It's not a holiday,' I whispered.

Shona leaned in and whispered back, 'What is it?'

'A mission.'

Shona's eyes widened. 'A mission? That sounds exciting!'

I thought of Neptune's nightmares, his fears. 'Hmm,' I said. 'Maybe. But listen – he's given us these shell phones. We can talk to each other with them. I want you to have mine.' I held out the shell for her. 'We've still got Aaron's to talk to Neptune, and you can call me on that one. Just say "silver" into the shell and Aaron's phone will light up.

Shona took the shell phone and turned it round in her hands. 'Really? You're sure?'

I nodded. 'For emergencies, OK?'

Shona closed her hand around the shell. 'Like if I'm missing you too much, or have some gossip that I absolutely *have* to share with you,' she said smiling.

I smiled back. 'Exactly!'

Shona laughed softly. 'No, I know it's not for that.

I probably won't use it. I don't want to get you into trouble. But I'm glad you gave it to me.'

'You're my best friend,' I said simply.

Shona smiled and threw her arms round my neck. 'You're the *best* best friend in the world,' she said.

I knew I wasn't, especially considering how much I'd neglected her lately. But I was really glad she still thought I was. I silently promised myself I would be a much better friend when this was all over.

Shona swished her tail and dived under the water. 'Come on,' she said. 'Let's go back to mine. I bet the crab cakes are done by now.'

And for the first time all week, as Shona and I swam along, chatting about all the trivial details of our lives, I briefly forgot about Neptune and his nightmares.

Friday morning came round far too quickly.

Neptune had told us to wait at the end of the pier. He'd organised a boat to pick us up and take us to where the cruise ship was waiting; it was one of those underwater pellet-shaped things that was half speedboat, half submarine. In any other circumstances, the adrenalin coursing through my blood would have been because of excitement. Not today. My body was shaking with nerves.

Aaron took my hand. 'It's going to be OK,' he said.

Mum was on the other side of me. She put her arm round my shoulders. 'Hey, cheer up, you two – anyone would think you were being sent off to war, not on a holiday!'

She had no idea how close to the truth she was.

'Yes, of course, ha ha,' I said, forcing a jolly laugh into my voice. 'I'm just sad to be leaving you.'

'Me too, sausage,' Mum said, giving me a squeeze. I could see how difficult she was finding it, and how hard she was trying not to show it. 'You'll be back soon enough though, won't you?'

'We'll be back before you know it!' Mr Beeston chipped in, coming up fast behind us. 'And don't worry,' he added. 'I'll be there to look after them all the time.'

We reached the end of the pier just as Dad popped his head up from under the water. 'It's here,' he said.

A moment later, the boat rose high enough for us to see a door open at the top.

I turned to give Mum one last hug and pretended not to notice the tear on her cheek wetting my own face as she held me close.

And then Aaron and I headed over to the ladder at the end of the jetty.

'COOOO-EEEEE! Hold on!'

I turned to see someone running down the jetty

towards us, a suitcase with clothes bursting out of it in her hand. Millie!

'Wait for me!' she shoutcd. 'I'm coming too!'

She caught us up, and, panting for breath, explained. 'Archie knows someone at the boat company and he managed to snag me a place! Isn't that great?'

'Well, yes, it's brilliant,' I said. 'But how come? I don't understand.'

'He's so well connected with his work. He said it was his gift to me because I've been under so much pressure lately.'

Millie had been under pressure? It was the first I'd heard of it.

'My bad dreams, and starting the new class and everything,' she explained stiffly, seeing my surprise. 'Anyway, you know how romantic he is — always surprising me with this, that and the other. So he arranged it. I just have to do a few tarot readings and a chakra session or two for the crew, and the captain said I can come!'

'Millie, that's wonderful,' Mum said. 'I'm glad you'll be there to keep an eye on them and make sure they're OK.'

Mr Beeston coughed pointedly.

'As well as the fine job that Mr Beeston will obviously be doing,' Mum added quickly.

'Hmm,' Mr Beeston said. 'I suppose it can't do any harm having two of us to watch them.'

'Exactly,' Millie beamed. 'Right, let's go.'

She passed her suitcase to Aaron and he clambered down the ladder with it above his head.

And then we were on the submarine, waving through the door at the top till Mum and Dad and Aaron's mum were specks in the distance.

A voice came over the loudspeaker. 'Everybody inside. Going under.'

We closed the door and took our seats down below.

This was it, then. After all the talking, the planning, the preparing – we were finally on our way to the world of Neptune's nightmares.

Chapter Six

I have to confess, I almost forgot about the whole dangerous mission thing once we'd left Neptune's submarine behind and boarded the cruise ship.

It was AMAZING! Easily the biggest boat I'd ever seen. It was more like a small town. There were eight levels, with balconies going all the way round on a couple of them, and a roof terrace with two hot tubs and a swimming pool. Inside the ship there was actually a lift that took you between decks! The restaurant served the biggest, poshest and most delicious meals you could think of. And the cabins – well, they weren't *huge*, but they were comfortable and clean.

I was sharing with Millie, and Aaron was sharing with Mr Beeston. As Millie's place had been so last minute, she'd actually been assigned a tiny cabin on the floor with all the staff. Millie being Millie, it hadn't taken her long to fix things so that she got to share my bigger one, with its porthole on the side, instead. I didn't mind. To be honest, it would have been a bit lonely on my own.

All in all, it was pretty fantastic. If we actually *had* been here for a holiday, I imagine it would have been the trip of a lifetime.

'Oooh, look at this one,' Millie said. She was flicking through the brochure of excursions that the company ran throughout the trip. 'Sea eagle safari. That sounds good, doesn't it?'

I sat down next to her on her bed and looked at the brochure over Millie's shoulder. *Journey with us into sea eagle territory – and don't forget your camera!* it read. There was a picture of about twenty people on a small boat, a giant eagle flying towards them with a fish in its talons. The eagle's eyes were black and hard. They seemed to be staring right off the page at me. I shivered. 'Not sure about that one,' I said.

'Quad bike safari?' Millie suggested, turning the page.

'Hmm, maybe.'

She flicked over another page. 'Glacier trip?'

My heart did a forward somersault into the air as I looked at the picture. The mountains, the lake, the glacier – I'd never seen them before, but I knew them.

It was the place that Neptune had described.

I tried to speak, but my throat suddenly had a large block of ice jamming it up. Instead, I just pointed at the picture and nodded.

Millie looked at me. 'You want to go on the glacier trip?'

'Mmm!' I said, nodding again.

'Not sure I fancy that one, myself,' she said. 'Maybe Mr Beeston can take you.' Then she licked a finger and turned the page, moving on to the rest of the excursions.

I cleared my throat and found my voice again. 'I'm going to see what Aaron's up to,' I said as casually as I could.

Millie closed the brochure. 'OK, dear,' she said. 'I might call Archie while you're gone.'

'Call Archie? What do you mean?'

Millie reached into her bag and fumbled around. Eventually, after pulling out packets of tissues, notebooks, pens and jars of strange-looking pills and scattering them across the bed, she found what she was looking for. A shell like the ones Neptune had given to Aaron and me – in shimmering green.

'Where did you get that?' I gasped.

'Archie gave it to me,' she said, hugging the shell. 'Said it would help to stop him missing me so much. It's magical, you see. We can talk to each other with it.'

'But how—'

'Oh, I know. He's a bit naughty, really. They're only meant to be used for top level emergencies. But he said us being apart *is* a top level emergency. He told me to call him and keep him up to date with what we're all doing. He's *so* romantic!' Millie sighed. 'He did say I should be careful about using it, though. He might get into trouble if we're caught using them just to whisper love messages to each other.'

I tried not to pull a face. I really didn't want to think too much about Millie and Archie's love messages.

'I suppose I shouldn't call him right now,' Millie sighed. 'Like he said, I'll wait till I really need to.'

With that, she kissed the shell and put it back in her bag.

'Right,' I said. 'I'll see you later.'

I left Millie to the rest of her unpacking and went to find Aaron. We'd only been apart for an hour to do our unpacking, and already I had so much to talk to him about: the glacier trip; Archie giving Millie one of those shells; in fact, him sneaking her onto the trip in the first place.

What exactly *was* Archie up to? The questions swam round in my head as I made my way to Aaron and Mr Beeston's cabin at the opposite end of the boat.

I bumped into Aaron in the corridor.

'I was just coming to see you!' we said in unison.

Aaron grabbed my hand and pulled me over to a couple of seats in a recess of the lounge. 'We need to talk,' he said. He had the excursions brochure on him. 'Look,' he said, opening it on the page I'd just been looking at.

'I've seen it,' I said.

'That's it, isn't it?'

I nodded. 'I'm pretty sure it is.'

Aaron pointed at the page. 'Have you seen the date of the trip?'

I followed his finger. My mouth fell open. 'But that . . . but that's . . .'

'I know,' Aaron said. 'It's tomorrow. We've got one night to prepare ourselves.'

'Listen to me.' Mr Beeston was doing his best to talk quietly as the three of us huddled in a corner of the ship, waiting for the small boat that was coming to take Aaron and me on the glacier trip.

'We haven't had a chance to talk properly yet,

and we haven't got much time now, but I need to tell you a few things.'

We leaned in and listened.

'I know this isn't a holiday,' Mr Beeston began. He looked searchingly at us both. What should we say? Admit he was right, or deny it? What if he was trying to trick us?

'Why do you say that?' Aaron asked carefully.

Mr Beeston tutted. 'Look, we don't have time to play games, so I'll tell you exactly what I know about my role. I'm not asking you for information. I'm here for you. All right?'

I nodded. 'All right.'

'Neptune has sent you both here for a reason. What, exactly, that reason is, I don't know. I am not privy to the details, and I am not asking you to tell me them. What I do know is that I am here to give you whatever support I can whilst you carry out your task to the best of your ability.'

'OK,' I said guardedly. 'Go on.'

'I know that you have to leave the ship and that I may have to cover for you while you are gone. I know that if there's anything you need from me, all you have to do is ask and, if I can provide it, I will.' He paused. 'And I know that if Neptune believes that the two of you are worthy of his trust and are up to the challenge he has set you – then I believe it, too.'

For a moment, I couldn't speak. My throat had

74

shrivelled up, and I think I must have got something in my eyes as they'd started watering.

He lowered his voice even further. 'And I know that it is here that you have to leave us.'

'How do you know that?' I asked.

'I didn't get to the position I hold today without learning how to read subliminal signals,' he said mysteriously.

Sub-what?

When we both looked at him blankly, he went on. 'Both of you look rigid with fear, and have done since this morning. It isn't rocket science.' He looked round at the holidaymakers smiling and laughing as they waited for the boat to come and take them out for the afternoon. Then he lowered his voice. 'You're not really here for the afternoon's glacier trip, are you?'

Aaron and I exchanged a look.

'OK, you're right,' Aaron said. 'We have to go to the glacier, but we're not sure where we have to go next. We have to . . .' He stopped and looked at me, then, reddening a touch, turned back to Mr Beeston. 'I don't know how much we can tell you,' he finished.

Mr Beeston waved a hand. 'It doesn't matter,' he said. 'I don't need to know. All *you* need to know is that I am covering your backs while you are gone. You have shell phones?'

Aaron pulled his out of his pocket. 'Yup,' he said.

I looked down and didn't say anything. I still

hadn't told Aaron I'd given mine to Shona. But as long as we had his, we'd be OK.

'I have one also,' Mr Beeston said. 'A blue one. Call me if you need me. I will do whatever I can to help.'

I could hardly believe I was thinking it, but for the first time in my life, I was glad to have Mr Beeston around. 'Thank you,' I said.

He smiled his wonky smile at me, and then he went on. 'The small boat will take you along the fjord.'

'What's a ford?' I asked.

'Fjord, not ford,' Mr Beeston corrected me. 'Say it as if it's spelt "fyord".'

'Fjord, then,' I said. 'What's one of those?'

'It's a narrow stretch of water, like a thin river. They are all over the place here, weaving in between the mountains and linking the lakes to the sea. After the boat drops you off at the end of the fjord, you'll catch the funicular train to the top of the mountains. You'll get the best views of the glacier from there, and hopefully see where you need to go next.'

'Thank you,' Aaron said.

'You know that the water here will be unbelievably cold. I presume Neptune has prepared you for this?'

I felt inside my pocket and closed my hand round the bottle Neptune had given us. 'We're prepared,' I said.

'And have you got any provisions?'

'I've got a couple of rolls and some fruit from the lunch buffet,' Aaron said.

'And I've brought a bottle of water,' I added.

'Right then,' Mr Beeston said, standing to attention so suddenly I almost thought he was going to salute us. Instead, he reached out a hand. For a moment, he looked as if he were going to shake our hands. Perhaps suddenly remembering that we were kids and not an elite and highly trained team of secret agents, he changed his mind and patted us both awkwardly on our arms.

'Neptune knows what he's doing,' he said. 'You'll be fine.'

I wasn't sure if I believed him on either of those statements, but as a large door opened on the side of the cruise ship and a smaller boat pulled alongside, I decided I would make his statements my mantra: *Neptune knows what he's doing. We'll be fine.*

If I repeated it over and over in my mind often enough, I might even end up believing it myself.

The small boat glided elegantly along the icy waters of the fjord: a river so tiny and so twisting it felt as if we were sailing through a hairline crack in the world. On either side, enormous mountains rose up into a perfect blue sky. Each of them was covered with a smattering of snow at the top, and alternating rocky drops and deep green forests down their sides.

Here and there, a waterfall ran through a crack between the mountains, gushing down and forking out at the bottom to spill into the water below. Next to these majestic mountains, even our huge ship looked tiny. I'd never seen anything like it, and for a moment I forgot what we were here for and let myself enjoy the view.

'Ready?' Aaron nudged me and pointed to a jetty ahead of us. Behind it, a steep pair of tracks and a wire above them led all the way up one of the mountains. 'Looks like this is our stop.'

The boat pulled up alongside the jetty and we all piled off and into the carriage that was waiting to take us up the mountain. Aaron and I sat near the front, gradually watching the world below us grow smaller and further away. We could see our boat in the distance; it looked like a toy. As the view of the fjords opened up, they looked like a giant's fingers stretching out across the land, reaching into crevices and cracks and tiny, winding hiding places.

Around us, people mingled and shuffled about, pushing past each other to take photos of the view. We sat, squashed tightly together, fingers entwined just as tightly, saying nothing.

At the top, everyone piled out of the carriage and dashed over to the viewing platform. We held back before making our way over to the other side of the summit.

Once we got there, the sight made me gasp. A stretch of water — another fjord — separated us from the range of mountains a short way away. The mountains looked as if they were set in a ring. The far one was covered in a glacier that looked like a giant's tongue reaching all the way down the mountain as though stretching out to take a lick from something — presumably a lake — down below. We couldn't see the lake itself from here, but we could see enough to know that this was the place Neptune had told us to find, and that the lake would be exactly where Neptune had said: in the centre of the mountains.

If I'd had any doubts about whether his dreams really were memories, they disappeared now, as I looked across at the glacier. I turned to Aaron. 'How are we going to get there?'

'We'll have to take one of the paths down this mountain first, then swim across the fjord. Maybe we'll find a break in the ring of mountains somewhere, and get to the lake.'

'And if we don't?'

'If we don't, I guess we'll have to try to climb over the top of one of the mountains. But let's worry about that when we get there, shall we?'

I nodded. We weren't exactly overwhelmed with options.

I looked round to see if anyone was watching us. Thankfully, they were all far too busy standing at the edge of the viewing platform taking photos of each other to notice us.

'Let's go,' Aaron said.

We edged away from all the people still milling about and squealing and pointing, and made our way to the edge of the summit. The path down looked straightforward enough – apart from the bottom part. From here, it looked as though the path ended a long way off the water. We'd probably have to jump the last bit.

As we picked our way down the rocky path, I prayed that Neptune's potion would work once we got into the sea. If it didn't, we'd both be dead from hypothermia in a matter of minutes.

'This is it, then.' Aaron's voice wobbled as we looked down at the clear blue water. It was the first time I'd seen him look nervous about getting into the sea. Normally he couldn't get in fast enough. But then, normally, he wasn't relying on a tiny glass vial filled with a magic potion to save him from fairly certain death.

'Come on,' I said. For once, I was first to the edge. I took out my bottle and jumped into the water. The shock of that first touch almost made my heart stop. But I forced myself to duck down. Teeth chattering so hard I thought my jaw was going to lock, I pulled the cork out of the bottle and tipped the fluid into my hands. As my tail formed, I spread the potion all over it. *Please work. Please work.*

For a second, nothing happened.

No! Neptune had given us the wrong thing! We were going to die!

But then I felt something change. I stopped panicking. It was working. My teeth had stopped chattering. My body warmed up. My tail flicked in the water. It had worked!

Moments later, Aaron was by my side. 'Phew!' he said. 'Glad that bit's over.'

We swam together to the other side of the fjord. The water was completely different from anywhere else I'd ever been. It was so clear it felt as if we were swimming through liquid glass, and the sea life was like nothing I'd seen before.

Strange jellyfish shaped like angels, with orange heads and fluorescent bodies, flickered up and down with tiny wings; red starfish lay on the sand below us, grouped together in bundles like a collection of wishes; weird see-through blobs that looked like light bulbs bounced towards us, bright yellow skeletons lighting up inside their bubbly bodies.

Huge flat rays with long tails skimmed the seabed, flicking their capes as they whizzed past us.

And it was so quiet. Everything moved silently. The only sound was the swishing of our tails as we made our way to the mountains.

Finally, we reached the other side. We pulled ourselves out of the water and sat on a small rocky beach while we waited for our legs to come back. My arctic-ready trousers returned with my legs, and I pulled my coat closer against the cold.

Aaron stood up first. 'Come on. Let's see if we can find a way through this mountain,' he said.

We trekked the length of the beach, looking for a way through the mountain. The water extended into crevices all along the coastline, but we couldn't see anything that seemed to go all the way through the mountain. All the caves were shallow. All the water trails ended in a wall. It was beginning to look as though we'd have to climb over the icy mountain after all. I wasn't sure I was up to it.

'Can we have a rest?' I asked. I sat down on a large flat rock in front of one of the sea-filled crevices.

'You're right. It's going to take all our energy to get up there,' Aaron said, sitting down beside me. 'We should recharge our batteries first.'

For some reason, talking about recharging batteries made me think about our shell phones. And the fact that I still hadn't told him about giving mine to Shona. Maybe this was a good moment.

'Aaron, I need to tell you something,' I said.

'Really? Me, too!' he replied. He looked oddly relieved. 'You first.'

'OK, so . . . um, you know how we were told not to tell anyone about this mission?'

Aaron nodded.

'Well, I haven't told anyone *all* the details, but I gave Shona my shell phone.' I didn't look at him in case he was angry. Instead, I went on quickly. 'I've hardly seen her lately because of, well, you and me. And I miss her, and I didn't want her to fall out with me so I wanted to give her something. I—'

'Emily.' Aaron put a hand on my arm. 'It's OK. I understand.'

'It is? You do?'

Aaron smiled. 'Of course I do. We've got my phone, anyway. Neptune never needs to know.'

I let out a breath. 'Thank you. You're so amazing and lovely!' I burst out before I could stop myself. Mainly to cover up my embarrassment at being so gushy, I added, 'So, what about you? What's the thing you have to tell me?'

Aaron shuffled awkwardly on the rock. His cheeks had reddened and he wouldn't look at me.

'Aaron?'

He fiddled with his hands in his lap. 'Look, I'm telling you because I don't want to keep anything from you, OK?'

'OK,' I said nervously.

'I didn't think anything of it at the time, but just. . . well, some things have happened that have made me wonder, and now I don't know what to think.'

'Aaron, what is it?' I was getting really worried now. 'Whatever it is, it'll be fine.'

'Promise?'

Could I really promise? 'Please, try me. You're scaring me.'

'Look it might be nothing . . .'

'Aaron, just tell me!'

'OK. Well, you remember the night of the concert?'

Did I remember the night of the concert? The night we brought the human and mer worlds together? The night Aaron kissed me? It was only the best night of my life! I wasn't going to forget that in a hurry!

'Yes,' I said with a shy smile. 'I remember.'

'Well, just before the concert, I had a weird conversation.'

'Who with?'

'With Archie.'

'*Archie?*'

'I didn't think of it as weird at the time,' Aaron went on quickly. 'But . . . well, have you noticed he's been acting a bit oddly lately?'

'Not half! What's up with him?'

'I don't know. But it made me think again about

the conversation. Especially with what Neptune told us – about our powers and everything.'

'Aaron, you're talking in riddles,' I said. 'What are you trying to tell me?'

Aaron carried on fumbling with his hands, and wouldn't look at me as he replied. 'He said I should kiss you.'

'He *what*?'

'He'd been teasing me about you for days, asking if you were my girlfriend and stuff.' Aaron's cheeks had flushed so deeply they were almost purple. 'I said I didn't really know. He said there was only one way to find out – that if I tried to kiss you, I'd know for sure if you felt the same way.'

'Go on,' I somehow managed to say through my tightly gritted teeth.

'He kept going on about it, joking and ribbing me, asking if I'd kissed you yet. Then, on the night of the concert, he said that it was the perfect time to do it. He even bet me that I wouldn't – said he'd give me a tenner if I did.'

I pulled myself up off the rock and moved away. I couldn't listen to this.

Aaron got up and followed me. 'Emily, wait!'

I turned to face him. 'You kissed me *for a bet*! There was me thinking what an amazing night it was – how romantic, how perfect – and all the time, you only did it to win ten pounds!'

'It wasn't really like that,' Aaron said.

Wasn't *really* like that? I wanted him to tell me it wasn't *at all* like that. But he didn't.

'You didn't do it because you *wanted* to,' I said. 'You did it because Archie pushed you into it. You had to prove what a big man you are. Well, I hope he paid up.' I turned on him and started to walk away. I slipped on a stone as I turned and Aaron laughed.

I stopped in my tracks. 'And you think it's *funny*?'

'No. It was just. Well, actually, it is *quite* funny, if you think about it,' Aaron said. 'I mean, I hadn't got round to – you know – doing it till then, and I suppose Archie did make me think about it.'

I stared at Aaron. 'So you hadn't even *thought* about kissing me till you were offered ten pounds to do it?'

I thought back to how *I'd* felt, how I'd been wanting to kiss him for weeks. If it was possible to die of shame and embarrassment, I would have dropped dead on the spot. I did the next best thing. I glared at Aaron and turned my shame into anger. 'Next time you're offered cash to make a fool of someone,' I snapped, 'it *won't* be me.'

'Oh, come on Emily! It's not the end of the—'

'I'm not listening.' I stomped off to the end of the scraggly beach and climbed some jagged rocks. How could he do that to me? How *could* he? And how could I have been such a fool? I'd thought we had something so special, and all the time he'd been laughing at me behind my back, kissing me for a *bet*!

I clambered over the rocks, desperate to get as far away from him as I could. I didn't want him to see my face – or the tears streaming down my cheeks. Angry tears. Not upset. Just angry.

On the other side of the rocks, there was another inlet. The tide had gone out further now and I clambered down from the rocks and paced across the pebbles.

It was halfway across them that I noticed the cave: taller than me and about three times my width, carved into the rock by years of tides crashing against it, and only exposed now that the tide had gone out.

I stepped inside it and peered into darkness. A few paces in, I was enveloped in the blackness – but the cave went on. Maybe it went all the way through the mountain. Maybe this was exactly what we'd been looking for!

The last thing in the *world* I wanted to do right then was go back and talk to Aaron – but we still had to complete the mission. And the quicker we got it over and done with, the sooner we'd be back home and I wouldn't have to have anything to do with him ever again.

I climbed back over the rocks. Aaron was standing

on the other side of them, throwing stones into the water.

He turned and saw me. 'Emily – please, let's stop this. It's stupid.'

Great. Now he was calling me stupid on top of everything else. I swallowed down a furious response and tried to gather as much dignity as I could. 'I don't want to talk about it,' I said calmly. 'I'm just glad that you've told me the truth so we both know where we stand.'

He opened his mouth to reply but I carried on before he got the chance to speak. 'In fact, I don't want to talk about anything with you except the mission. Let's just get on with the job we're here to do, and forget about everything else. OK?'

Aaron just stared at me. I wondered what he was thinking. If he argued with me now, if he begged me to listen, told me it was all a big mistake, I would forgive him on the spot. If he didn't – well, that would just confirm I was doing the right thing.

Aaron sighed heavily. 'OK,' he said.

I hid my desperate disappointment. It was settled, then. I hadn't got it wrong. Aaron *had* kissed me for a bet and it *had* meant nothing to him. Well, it was a good thing I knew. It was time to put it behind me and get on with our mission.

'Good,' I said, clipping any emotion from my voice. 'Now, follow me. I think I've found a way through the mountain.'

We crept through the tunnel. Aaron led the way. The further we went, the darker it got. If it hadn't been for what had just happened, I'd have jumped at the excuse to hold his hand and get as close as possible. As it was, I kept my distance, zipped my mouth as tight as my coat and plodded on through the damp, cold blackness.

Just as I was beginning to wonder if we should give up and turn round, Aaron's voice echoed back to me.

'Look!'

I peered into the murky darkness. What was I meant to be looking at?

'Ahead!' Aaron called. 'Light.'

He was right. I could just about see a tiny pinprick of light. The hope spurred us on and we sped up, trudging through the watery, echoey tunnel.

Gradually, the pinprick of light turned into a small circle. Then it grew to the size of a football. Eventually, it opened up so much that we could see out. We'd done it! We'd got through the mountain!

Once we were nearly out in the open again, Aaron turned to me. 'We did it!' he said, coming towards me with his arms wide open.

'What are you doing?' I said, folding my arms.

He dropped his arms. 'I thought we—'

'Well, you thought wrong!' I snapped. 'You think I'm just going to forget everything you've told me and go running into your arms as though it never happened? As though I'll *ever* trust you again?'

Aaron just stood looking at me, his cheeks red as though I'd slapped him. I had to turn away, but I wasn't backing down. *He* was the one in the wrong here, not me.

'Let's just get on with what we're here to do,' I said more gently. 'And forget the rest of it for now. OK?'

Aaron nodded glumly. 'OK.'

We picked our way across the last bit of scraggly ground at the tunnel's entrance, to come out into the daylight. I rubbed my eyes and looked around.

The view was utterly breathtaking. All around us, mountains stood majestically in the bright light of the afternoon. Their tops were sprinkled with snow, as though someone had carelessly tipped icing sugar all over them.

A low cloud cut the top off one of the mountains, sitting above it like a hat. Another had waterfalls tumbling from about halfway up where the snow ended, all the way down, splitting into five different channels so sharp and white they looked like forked lightning.

And in the centre of the ring of peaks – a lake.

Around the base of all the mountains, the colour

of the rock was different. The whole bottom section was a deep reddy brown. It looked like a tide mark, like the lake used to be much higher than it was now.

We took a few steps towards the lake. I'd never seen such still water in my life. If someone had told me that it was actually a round mirror and not a lake at all, I would have believed them. Not a thing moved. The water lay silent, the mountains stood hushed and protective around it.

High up, an eagle flew from a tree and came swooping towards us as if checking on intruders. It came so close I saw its beady black eyes – and then it swooshed away again. The silence returned.

I took a few more steps towards the edge of the lake and looked down. The mountains looked back up at me, the clouds floated perfectly still around them, like white fluffy islands in the sky.

Aaron was beside me. 'I thought the reflection was meant to be different,' he said. 'Neptune said it wouldn't be the same as the reality.'

I turned in a circle, examining the mountains, then looked back down. That was when I spotted it.

'It isn't!' I breathed. 'Look.' I pointed at the reflection in the water. 'See the two mountains there with all the snow, and then that huge tall one in between them?'

Aaron followed where I was looking. 'I see it,' he said.

I turned and pointed up towards the mountains. 'Now look,' I told him.

Aaron gasped as he gazed where I was pointing. The two mountains were there, snow-capped exactly the same as their reflections in the lake. But there was no third mountain between them.

'But that's—'

'Impossible?'

'Exactly.'

The third mountain – the one we could see clearly reflected in the lake – it didn't exist.

Which was when I knew without doubt that we were in the right place.

Chapter Seven

I stood at the water's edge, looking down and trying to work out how the reflection of the third mountain could be possible. The fact was, it *wasn't* possible. And yet, it was here in front of our eyes. Not only that, but it had been predicted, too. Neptune had told us we would see this.

So now what?

Aaron was beckoning me over. 'Em, you have to look at this.'

I went to see what he was staring at. He pointed

into the water right in front of us. 'Look at my reflection,' he said.

I followed his finger. His reflection was pointing right back at him.

'What about it?' I asked.

'Watch my eyes.'

I looked at his eyes in the water. They were darting here, there, everywhere, looking round at the mountains, staring up from the lake into the blue sky above us, glancing this way and that.

'Stop looking around so much,' I said.

'But that's just it. I'm not.'

I turned to face him, and watched him as he looked down into the lake. He was staring straight down at his reflection. I looked back at the Aaron in the lake; the eyes were still darting about everywhere.

'But I don't understand,' I murmured.

'You try it,' Aaron said. 'Try to look into your own eyes.'

I looked straight down at myself – but I couldn't meet my own gaze. My reflection's eyes were darting all over the place, just like Aaron's.

'Remember what Neptune said about the lake?' Aaron asked. 'He said you have to meet your own eyes.'

'But we can't,' I said.

Aaron hesitated. Then he mumbled, 'What if we hold hands?'

Suddenly I was cross. 'Have you done this?' I asked.

'Done what?'

I pointed at the lake. 'This. You've done some kind of trick. Probably one that Archie taught you. I don't know how you've done it, but if you think you can make a fool of me again, you can forget it!' I snapped.

'Emily! Listen to yourself. You're being ridiculous. Of *course* I haven't done a trick.' And before I could stop him, Aaron had reached out and grabbed my hand. I tried to pull away, but he held on too tightly.

'Look,' he said. With his other hand he was pointing at the lake.

Our reflections were shimmering, as though the water had been disturbed, ripples blurring the edges of our bodies. Nothing else in the lake moved.

'Meet your eyes,' Aaron said.

I looked down at myself. My image looked right back into my eyes. I stopped struggling against Aaron's hand, and turned to him. 'Now what?' I asked.

Aaron shrugged. 'I don't know. Why don't we try doing it together? We each look into our own eyes at the same time?'

'OK.'

I met my eyes, staring down at myself, knowing Aaron was doing the same, and trying to ignore the feeling of a thousand moths fluttering in my chest. Within seconds, the eyes staring back at me turned black.

'Aaron!'

'Keep holding on,' he said firmly. 'And keep looking.'

I stared into the black holes where I should have been seeing eyes. The blackness grew, sending the water spinning as it did so. Soon it had taken over my whole face, now my body, now it had joined with the blackness coming from Aaron's reflection, too. Within a couple of minutes, we were staring into a spinning, fizzing black whirlpool that had stolen both our reflections.

Neptune's words were ringing in my ears. *You must meet your eyes and jump.*

'You know what we have to do, don't you?' Aaron asked.

I nodded. 'Ready?'

'Don't let go of my hand,' Aaron said.

'I won't,' I replied reluctantly.

Aaron took a breath. 'OK, one, two, three . . . go!'

Still holding hands, and with no idea what we were getting ourselves into, we took a breath – and jumped.

For the first few seconds, the water was so cold I wondered if Neptune's potion had worn off, but as my tail formed, my body warmed.

In the shock of the cold, I'd dropped Aaron's hand. But now we were actually in the lake it didn't seem to matter. Maybe once we'd jumped in, we'd broken the spell.

The water was so clear I could see the mountains through the surface of the lake.

Aaron was looking around. 'Now what?'

I shook my head. 'No idea. Have a look around?'

We swam through the lake, looking for anything that might give us a clue to our next move. But apart from an occasional lone fish, long see-through tubes of seaweed and tiny bits of ice dotted about like tiny crystals, there was nothing.

'Look at this,' Aaron said. In front of us, the water looked as if it were swirling round in a whirlpool. But as I got closer, I could see it wasn't a whirlpool at all; it was hundreds of bubbles.

That was when I realised – they were everywhere. Tiny little bubbles the size of raindrops; bigger ones that looked like those Mum and I used to make by squeezing the washing-up liquid bottle while we were doing the dishes; bigger ones still, the size of footballs, beach balls, even the big medicine balls you get in the gym.

'Do you think we can touch them?' I asked.

In reply, Aaron swam towards a medium-sized bubble and held his hand against it. 'Yuk! It feels like slime. Gooey, sticky slime.'

I swam over and joined him. 'Here,' I said, holding out my hand. 'Take it.'

Aaron smiled broadly and grabbed hold of my hand.

'And before you get any ideas, no I haven't forgiven you,' I said.

His smile dropped, but he held on firmly to my hand.

Together, we swam towards one of the bubbles. Still holding hands, we each placed our other hand on the bubble. Aaron was right about it feeling weird. It felt a bit like putting my hand on cold, stale custard. But I didn't get to spend very long thinking about how it felt. The bubble shimmered and glistened for a second, and then something started to form inside it: pictures, people.

Aaron and I stared into the bubble. A middle-aged couple were standing in a room together, a sofa along one side, a television in the corner. The television was on, but they weren't watching it. It looked as though they were arguing.

'They're speaking,' Aaron said. 'Listen.'

Still pressing my hand against the bubble, I moved closer and tried to tune in to the sounds.

'I'm telling you, I saw it with my own eyes! Ask Mr Barrett if you don't believe me,' the man was saying. His face was bright red, his voice raised and high-pitched.

His wife stood shaking her head, her arms folded across her chest. 'And exactly how long did you and Mr Barrett spend in The Ship Inn before your fishing trip?' she asked through tightly pursed lips.

The man sighed. 'I've told you. We had half a pint, that's all. It was nothing to do with that. It was real. We both saw it – a mermaid.'

I jumped away. I felt as if the words had leapt out of the bubble and touched me, snapping electric shocks into my skin. A mermaid? They were talking about mermaids! What *was* this?

'Let's try another one,' I said.

We held hands again and swam towards another bubble, a smaller one this time. Again, we put our hands on the bubble. Instantly it exploded into a vision – a mini drama playing out in front of our eyes.

Two children on a beach. A little girl of about six or seven with a boy maybe half her age.

'Mummy, Mummy!' The little girl called as she ran up the beach. 'I saw a mermaid!'

The boy toddled behind her. 'I saw a err daid!' he squealed delightedly.

And then it was gone. The vision was finished.

Aaron and I looked at each other. Neither of us had any words. He pulled me towards another bubble – a larger one this time. We did it again, held hands, placed our free hands on the bubble. The scene began: two women at a table, both maybe in their twenties. One of them was hunched over the table, her head in her arms. 'I can't bear it!' she cried. 'Where is he? What have they done with him?'

There was something familiar about the woman's voice.

She looked up at the other lady, her face turned away from us. 'And what will happen to my baby?' she wailed. It was only when she said this that I noticed the cot beside the table. A tiny baby was fast asleep, wrapped in a white blanket.

The other woman put a hand on her friend's shoulder. 'Whatever happens, I'm here for you,' she said. 'I'll look after you. That's what best friends are for.'

Wait! *Her* voice was familiar too!

The woman got up from the table and put her arms round her friend. 'Thanks, Millie,' she said. 'I don't know what I'd do without you.'

Millie? My hand, still on the bubble, started shaking. The image began to blur.

'Oh, don't be silly. You'd survive. And listen, we *will* find Jake.'

Jake? My dad?

The two women pulled away from the hug. The woman who had been crying wiped her eyes and turned in our direction. And then I was left in no doubt whatsoever. This was a twenty-something version of my mum! And the tiny baby sleeping beside her – I guess that was me.

My hands were shaking so much the image blurred beyond recognition.

'Aaron, I don't like this,' I said. 'I don't understand. What is this place?'

Aaron swam round to face me. 'I don't know,' he said. 'They seem to be scenes from the past.'

'Well, I'd figured that much out!' I snapped.

'Em, please, can we just . . .' He touched my arm. I flinched.

'Can we just what?'

He hesitated for ages, till I had to look at him. 'Can we just put the other stuff to one side for now?' he said. 'Can we be friends?'

Friends? Was that what we were? Was that all he had ever wanted to be? What we'd have been all along if he hadn't been egged on by a bet?

'I don't know if I want to be your friend,' I said.

'Can we at least try? For the sake of this mission? Please?'

He was right. This was all going to be hard enough without us being at each other's throats. And after what I'd just seen, I certainly felt in need of a friend, right now. 'OK, we'll try,' I mumbled.

Aaron's face broke out into such a big smile that for a moment I wished he'd never told me about that stupid bet. I wished I could just carry on telling myself how happy we were. Maybe ignorance *was* bliss.

'OK, so I've got a theory,' he said.

'Go on.'

'I think they're memories.'

'Of course! Each of the bubbles is a separate memory.'

'Every time someone had a memory taken away,' Aaron waved an arm around him at all the bubbles, 'it became a new bubble here in this lake!'

'A lake of lost memories,' I said.

'Exactly.'

Then I remembered something. 'But Neptune undid the memory drug. People have had their memories returned to them.'

'Not everywhere – only in Brightport.'

'But my mum's in Brightport.'

Aaron thought for a moment. 'Maybe it was so long ago, and so painful, that she never got that memory back.'

It all made sense. As much sense as the idea of a lake full of lost memories could make, anyway. Mum *was* super-forgetful. There was every chance that, even though the memory drug had been lifted, some really old memories were still locked away.

Then I had another thought. 'The tide mark on the mountains!'

'What about it?'

'That must be because of the memories that have come back.'

'You're right! As people's memories are returned, the lake empties out a bit more,' Aaron said.

'So if this lake holds everyone's forgotten memories, perhaps the ones that were taken from Neptune are in here somewhere.'

'Come on,' Aaron said. 'Let's find them!'

'How?'

'Hmm, that's a thought. I've got no idea.'

'Why don't we look for bubbles that stand out in some way?' I suggested. 'Surely Neptune's memories will look bigger and grander than all the others.'

'Good idea.' Aaron hesitantly put his hand out.

I hesitantly put mine out to meet it. 'We're just friends, remember,' I said tightly.

We held hands and went in search of the biggest, grandest bubbles we could find.

After a few more random mermaid memories, we found a huge bubble – it was almost as big as me.

'Ready?' Aaron asked. We stretched our arms out so we could hold hands and get our other hand around it as it bounced and swayed in front of us.

'Ready.'

I placed my hand on the bubble. Instantly, the scene opened up: a tall, bearded merman with a frown on his face and piercing, angry eyes. He looked ragged and tired.

'Neptune!' I whispered.

'Found it!' Aaron whispered back.

Neptune's angry eyes creased up, as though he were in pain. 'Help me! HELP ME! Please – it's unbearable! Hurry – please, hurry! It will be too late soon.' He stretched out his arms, as though begging someone. Whoever he was talking to was too far away to see, though. Neptune was the only one in the picture.

'Stop this. You have to stop it!' His voice was so anguished it tore at me. I could hardly bear to listen. 'Don't let him have it,' Neptune growled. 'DO NOT let him have it. The narwhal – bring it to me. He can't have it or it will be too late for us all. No one will ever mend this. Please! HURRY!'

The image faded away. We let go of each other's hands and swam away.

'What on earth was that about?' Aaron asked.

'Search me.' I glanced around. 'Look, there's another big bubble over there. Shall we try it?'

We swam across the lake and a flicker of nerves swam through my stomach, just like the shoal of bright yellow fish that danced along beside me. What would we see this time?

Once again, we held hands, touched the bubble and watched as the scene emerged in front of our eyes.

It was Neptune again. This time, he looked even worse. Deep black rings surrounded his eyes; his hair was lank and lifeless. He was thin, barely moving. His face was as white as the snow at the top of the mountains surrounding the lake.

Again, he was talking to someone out of the picture.

'Go to the mountain with the hole in the top, and wait,' he was saying. 'Under the midnight sun, the ice will melt. Catch that water in your hands.' His face hardened into the frown we had seen so many times in real life. 'It is my birthright!' he snarled. 'Bring it to me!'

The image faded and the bubble went dark. A moment later, a new picture opened up. Neptune again, with another merman in front of him. The merman was talking. 'I couldn't catch it. I tried, but I couldn't hold it. The water burned my hands.' He held out his hands as he spoke. They were red and raw, and blistered all the way up to his wrists. 'I'm sorry,' he said. 'I'm so sorry.'

Again the image faded to black. We waited again. Gradually, the blackness lifted to a dull grey. Amongst the grey, I could just see Neptune, but this time it was only his outline, as though he was fading away. 'It's over,' he said, his voice echoing and bouncing around the edges of the bubble. He sounded like he was talking to himself. Had he gone mad? 'They have all either forgotten or frozen. No one is left to save me. I'm doomed . . . There is nothing . . . No one . . .'

The image faded to blackness and this time no new scene replaced it.

I let go of Aaron's hand and looked around. We were still surrounded by bubbles, but I couldn't see any more of the larger ones. To be honest, I was quite relieved. I wasn't sure how many more of these distressing scenes I could take.

Something terrible had clearly happened to Neptune. No wonder his memories had made him so scared, but what were we meant to do about it? How would we ever make sense of all this?

'OK, let's look at what we've got,' Aaron said. 'What were the main things we saw here? What were the main things we heard?'

'Neptune in a state,' I said. 'In fact, in about three different states, and each one worse than the one before.'

'What else?'

'Something about water.'

'Yes,' Aaron said. 'Something to do with catching water in your hands, and the midnight sun.'

'And something about a hole in the top of a mountain.'

'What was that thing Neptune said to bring him?'

'A wall or something,' I said

'Yeah, a nar wall, I think it was. What's one of those?'

I shook my head. 'I have absolutely no idea.'

'OK, so how about if we start by looking for the mountain with the hole in the top?' Aaron suggested.

To be honest, looking for a mountain with a hole in the top didn't sound like the easiest thing in the world to do, but, as I didn't have any better suggestions, it was as good a place to start as any.

I turned and started swimming. 'OK, let's give it a go. What have we got to lose?'

As we made our way to the edge of the lake, I didn't really want to think too hard about that question, just in case the answer was 'everything'.

Chapter Eight

We swam to the edge of the lake and pulled ourselves out. Sitting on a cold, rocky beach, we watched our tails flick and twitch, and finally felt our legs return.

'The glacier is that way,' I said, pointing to the far end of the lake where the icy giant's tongue spilled all the way down the mountain, almost to the water. 'I reckon that's where we need to start.'

'How do you figure that out?' Aaron asked.

'If we have to find water out of a mountain,

it makes sense that it's going to come from the glacier.'

Aaron stood up. 'Good thinking,' he said, and we made our way towards the glacier.

I don't know if you've ever tried climbing up a glacier without ice picks, ropes, or the tiniest bit of instruction on how to do it, but let me tell you – it isn't easy. In fact, it was impossible.

'We're never going to do this,' Aaron complained after slipping and falling on his backside for the fifth time.

In any other circumstances, I would have laughed. He did look quite comical. But two things stopped me: a glance at his angry, red face and the fact that I had also fallen, in an equally ungraceful manner, at least as many times.

I suppose the knowledge that we were on a highly dangerous, risky mission possibly took a bit of humour out of the situation, too.

'OK, let's try something different,' I said after slipping and landing awkwardly yet again.

'What do you suggest?'

I looked around. 'Perhaps we need to find a way round the glacier, instead of trying to climb up it.'

'I wonder how deep the ice is,' Aaron said. 'Does it go all the way inside, or is the mountain still there underneath?'

'Of course! That's it!'

'That's what?'

'We've been thinking we have to search the outside of it,' I said. 'But if there's a hole in the top, maybe it goes all the way down. It could join up with a tunnel inside the mountain.'

'Like the one we came through to get here?'

'Exactly! If we can find a tunnel like that which goes through the mountain with the glacier, we might find the hole from inside it.'

Aaron didn't look convinced.

I frowned. 'Have you got any better ideas?'

'No,' he said quickly. 'I think it's a great idea. Let's go.'

An hour later, we hadn't found anything. I flopped down on a rock at the foot of the mountain. The lake came right up to the edge at this point, lapping against the smooth, round boulders. 'OK, maybe that wasn't such a clever idea.'

'It was worth a try, though,' Aaron said, coming to sit with me on the rocks.

I looked down at the water. It was so clear I

could almost see the bottom. The edge of the lake tapered into a scraggly v-shape in the rocks which disappeared into darkness.

Wait!

'Aaron, I've had an idea,' I said, jumping down from the rock. 'We need to get back in the lake.'

Aaron looked at me doubtfully.

'Look at that dent in the rocks.' I pointed back to where we'd been sitting. 'It gets wider just under the surface.'

Aaron's eyes brightened as he caught on to what I was saying. 'Of course! The tunnel through the mountain might be underwater!' Aaron smiled. 'What are we waiting for?' He jumped back into the water.

As soon as our tails had formed and we'd shaken off the icy cold, we explored the rocks all around the edge of the lake. Eventually, we found something: a crack that would have been barely visible above the water line, but which opened up into a narrow tunnel just below it.

We swam into the tunnel.

We were soon swimming in pitch darkness. The tunnel snaked through the rock, twisting this way and that, narrowing in places before widening out again.

We swam close to the surface, but after a while I could feel the sandy ground below me. The water was getting shallower with every swish of my tail. And we still hadn't found a hole in the top of the mountain.

We swam on, my tail brushing against sand and rocks, until it was too shallow to swim. In pitch blackness, we waited, beached on the sand until our tails fizzed away and our legs came back.

I stood up, reaching around me to get a sense of where we were. I'd got used to the darkness enough to be able to see the edges of the damp, rocky tunnel. The roof was a little way above my head. I could just about see Aaron in front of me. He had to stoop slightly so he didn't bump his head on the tunnel's rocky ceiling.

'Now what?' he asked.

'Let's keep going,' I said. 'It's got to lead somewhere.'

So we trudged on, through the dark, cold, echoey belly of the mountain – and tried to hold on to a belief that this was going to lead us to any kind of answer.

It felt as though we'd been walking for hours when something began to change. I didn't even realise what it was at first. All I knew was that I'd suddenly become aware of different shades in the stony walls. Long, squiggly green lines trailed the length of the rock, like veins running along someone's arm. Odd shapes hung down from the ceiling – stalactites shaped like ice-cream cones and daggers and fans.

'Aaron!' I burst out. 'Look!'

He turned round. I could see his face clearly: a graze above his left eye where he must have hit a rock; black dusty muck all over his cheeks.

'What?' he asked. Then his eyes widened. 'I can see you!' he said.

'Exactly! There's light coming in from somewhere.'

We carried on with renewed energy and purpose. Light could only mean one thing. Well, two things. Either we were coming out on the other side of the mountain, or there was a hole letting the light in.

Sure enough, a few minutes, a few more twists and turns, and a lot more light later . . .

'Wow!' Aaron said. The tunnel had opened up, widening into a circle the size of a small room. Right in the centre, a thick shaft of dusty sunlight beamed down from above like a spotlight on a stage.

We'd found the hole in the top of the mountain.

Except it wasn't a complete hole. It went all the way up through the mountain, right from where we were – which I guessed was the very centre – up as high as the mountain itself had looked from outside. But we couldn't see the sky. Over the top of the hole was a layer of ice – the underside of the glacier.

'Now what?' I asked, looking into the shaft of light.

'I think we just need to wait.'

'Wait? What for?'

Aaron checked his watch. 'For about three hours to pass,' he said.

'Huh?'

He twisted his arm round to show me his watch. 'It's just gone nine o' clock,' he said. 'Remember what Neptune said in that bubble?'

'Under the midnight sun, the ice will melt.'

'So we just need to wait till midnight, catch the water in our hands and then ...' Aaron's voice faded. 'And then ... um ...'

'And then we have no idea,' I said.

Aaron grimaced. 'Yeah, pretty much.'

'Maybe once we've got the water, we'll have some idea of what to do with it.'

'At least we've got three hours to think about it,' he said.

I perched on a big, rocky stalagmite and tried not to feel too despondent. If it hadn't been for what Aaron had told me about his bet, I would have relished the thought of three hours on my own with Aaron, snuggled up against the cold and the damp. As it was, I sat as far away from him as I could without being too pointed about it, and hoped the hours would pass quickly.

We sat and listened to the sounds of the cave. A tiny *drip, drip, drip* echoed from deep in the tunnel. The rocks themselves seemed to hum, a low, damp, living noise. Every now and then, there was a shuffling, scurrying sound of something running about in the darkness. I didn't even want to think what that 'something' might be.

'Em,' Aaron said after a little while. 'You know that stuff with Archie . . .'

'Aaron, I don't want to talk about it,' I said. 'Not when we've got all this to deal with.' I couldn't bear the thought of him going over it again. Just thinking about his bet with Archie felt like a knife going through me. I didn't want to be stabbed with the same thing over and over again.

'But Emily!' Aaron burst out. 'It was only a stupid kiss!'

'A stupid kiss?' The knife stabbed at me again.

'I mean a stupid bet,' Aaron said grumpily. 'What's the difference? Either way, it's all ruined now. And you're probably right.'

'Right about what?'

'About us just being friends.' He looked at me

and his voice softened a tiny bit. 'I mean, if that's what you want, too?'

Was he giving me the chance to suggest we try again? Or just checking that I agreed with him about us being friends? I couldn't take the risk. I wasn't going to put my heart out there for him to trample on. I couldn't trust him.

I tried for a bright smile. 'Yes it is,' I lied, determined to do it convincingly. 'I mean, look at us now. We're getting on OK. We're doing the job really well. I *like* it like this.' I forced an even bigger, brighter smile onto my face. I hoped it didn't look too much as though someone was trying to stretch my mouth so wide that it could hang off my ears. That was certainly how it felt. But there was no way I was going to let him see I wanted anything more. Not now that he'd made it perfectly clear he didn't.

'You're sure?' Aaron asked.

'Mm hm,' I said.

He looked relieved. 'OK then,' he said. 'That's what we'll do.'

I got up and turned away. I couldn't bear him to see any hint of my real feelings behind my big, false smile: the hurt at not being his girlfriend, and the anger that he was clearly fine with the idea.

'Good. I'm glad that's settled,' I said sharply. I brushed my legs down. They were dusty from the rocks. 'I'm just going to have a little look around. I'll be back in a bit.'

'D'you want me to come with you?'

I shook my head 'No, you stay here. I won't be long.'

I turned my back and set off to explore the cave a bit further – and tried to banish the tears that were threatening to spill from my eyes at any moment.

Eventually, after what felt like days of waiting, it was nearly midnight. We'd eaten all our provisions and almost drunk all the water. My stomach was grumbling and my legs were aching from sitting around on cold rocks for hours.

We stood on the edge of the shaft of dusty light, waiting to see what would happen. The seconds ticked slowly by until it was a minute to midnight. My heart was thumping fast.

'You OK?' Aaron asked.

'Fine,' I said. 'You?'

He nodded. 'I just hope this is going to work.'

'Yeah, me too.'

And then we waited in silence for one more minute, until, finally, midnight arrived.

The first thing I noticed was the creaking, squeaking sound from way, way above our heads.

'Look!' Aaron was pointing upwards. 'It's happening. The midnight sun – it's melting the ice!'

'Now all we have to do is catch it as it falls.' I had the feeling that might not be as easy as it sounded.

A moment later, the first drip came. Plopping down right in the centre of the dusty shaft of light, it bounced with a loud *PLINK!* on the floor, and rebounded to scatter a tiny rainbow around the cave. A second later, the rainbow had gone, and the chamber was silent again.

'Wow!' Aaron said. 'That was a bit—'

PLINK!

Another drip, just like the first, landing on the ground and trickling away as quickly as it had come.

'Hey, I was trying to—'

PLINK!

Aaron gritted his teeth. 'Come on, we need to catch one of these,' he said. Kind of stating the obvious.

I tried reaching out to catch the drips, but kept missing them. They didn't drop in the exact same spot each time, so it was hard to judge where the next one was going to fall.

Aaron stepped into the centre of the light and held out both hands.

I held my breath and waited. The next drip landed right in his outstretched palms!

'Yes!' he yelled. And then a split second later, he leapt out of the light, clutching his hand, doubled over. 'Argghh! It's burning me!' He was jumping around, waving his hand about. 'It's burning! It's burning!'

'Quick, over here.' I dragged him to a narrow part of the cave that I'd discovered earlier where there was a small rock pool in the middle of a few boulders. Aaron shoved his hand in the water and instantly calmed down.

After a few moments, he took his hand out. It was red and raw, skin peeling off his palm, blisters already forming.

'What happened?' I asked.

Aaron shook his head. 'It's not just ordinary water. It's got some kind of magic in it. Remember that memory we saw in the lake? That servant telling Neptune he'd tried to catch the water and burned himself?'

I pulled the water bottle out of my pocket. 'Let's try catching it in this,' I suggested.

'Neptune told the servant he had to catch it in his hands.'

'But we can't,' I insisted. 'So this has got to be worth a try.'

'OK. But let me do it.' Before I could argue, Aaron took the bottle and stood in the centre of the shaft of light again. Within seconds, a drip came. He caught it in the bottle on his first attempt.

'Did it!' he said, smiling as he held the bottle out to show me.

His smile faded as we both looked at the bottle. The water had burned all the way through the plastic, scorching a hole in it.

Aaron's face looked as ragged as his fingers. I wanted to take his hand in mine. I wanted to kiss it better. I quickly moved away, before I was tempted to do either.

And then it hit me. The thing about taking Aaron's hand in mine – and about the magic. Of *course*! How could we have been so stupid?

'Aaron! We have to do it together!'

'No way!' Aaron said straight away. 'I'm not letting you go through this. It's awful!' I looked at him. Maybe he did care about me, after all. Just a bit.

I brushed the thought away, in case I found myself believing it. 'We have to do it while holding hands,' I said. 'It's magic isn't it? Neptune's magic. If we hold hands, maybe we can catch the water safely.'

Aaron thought for a moment. 'I don't know. This is really, really painful. If anything like this happened to you, I'd—'

'Aaron, we haven't got any choice,' I said. '*You* haven't got any choice. I'm doing it. Come on.'

He followed me back to the light. The drips had

slowed. 'We'll have to be quick,' I said. 'We don't know how long it's going to carry on.'

I gently took hold of his burned hand. 'Hold the other one out,' I said. 'Come on, we can do it together. You know we can.'

Eventually, he nodded reluctantly. 'OK,' he said.

We both took a breath, then we stepped into the light, held out our hands and waited.

Chapter Nine

I looked up through the mountain's vertical tunnel. Above me, the sky was a dusty blue, the sun's light dancing around the edges of the hole, burning through the ice, making the hole bigger and bigger. I still couldn't get my head round the fact that it was midnight and the sun was shining.

And then, almost in slow motion, I saw it – the drop of water falling towards us. I tightened my grip on Aaron's hand. 'It's coming,' I said. He looked up and tightened his grip, too. Between us, our outstretched hands made one big cup.

The drip fell directly into our palms.

I took a sharp breath, waiting for the searing pain. But it didn't come. Instead, the drip of water rolled around in our hands, hardening, turning back into ice, then crystallising into something more beautiful. It finally came to rest on my palm.

'Wow, it looks like a diamond or something,' Aaron said.

I stared at the crystal, entranced by its beauty.

'Look – another one!'

I glanced up just in time to see the second drip land in our palms. This time it rolled into Aaron's hand, crystallising and sparkling just as mine had done.

It happened once more, until we ended up holding three small crystals. We waited another few minutes, but no more drips came.

'I reckon that must be it,' Aaron said. 'It's past midnight now.'

'Should we try letting go?' I asked.

Aaron nervously bit his lip. 'I suppose we'll have to at some point,' he said.

Unfortunately, I thought. Not that I would have said that out loud – not now, anyway.

'Let's put the crystals away somewhere first,' I said. 'At least that way if the magic dissolves as soon as we let go, they won't burn our hands. I'll take them.' Aaron gave me his crystal and I zipped the three of them into my coat pocket. I turned to him. 'Ready?'

'Ready,' Aaron said.

I held my breath as we dropped each other's hands.

Nothing happened. I patted my pocket to see if the crystals were still there, and they were. They were safe and, more to the point, so were we.

'Right, let's get out of here,' Aaron said.

'Good idea.' I looked around. Looked left, looked right, straight ahead, behind us. It all looked the same. There were tunnels everywhere. Identical routes – each one leading in a different direction.

'Which way?' I asked, trying not to panic.

Aaron pointed down a tunnel. 'That way,' he said confidently. Then he added, a bit less certainly, 'I think.'

I set off in the direction he'd suggested. 'We might as well try it,' I said. 'If it's wrong, we can always come back and try one of the others.'

Aaron followed me. Soon we were back in total darkness. How we were ever going to know if this was the right direction was anyone's guess.

But then something weird happened. There was a faint glow coming from somewhere nearby. Was there another hole above us?

I looked up. Nothing.

Then, looking down, I saw it. It was my pocket – it was glowing with light. The crystals!

I pulled one of them out, and it was as though I'd lit a candle. It gave us enough light to see a little way ahead. We carefully made our way through the tunnel as I held the crystal in front of me like an old-fashioned oil lamp.

We'd been walking for quite a while when Aaron stopped. 'I don't think this is right,' he said. 'We had more twists and turns than this on the way in.'

'Are you sure?'

'No, not sure.'

'What d'you want to do?'

'I suppose it's a bit of a waste to have come all this way and then turn back – especially if we're not sure it's the wrong path,' Aaron agreed. 'Let's try going a bit further.'

We walked on in silence for a while. But the more we walked, the more I began to think Aaron was right. This felt wrong. It wasn't just that it didn't feel like the same route we'd taken coming in, there was more to it than that: a sense that we were moving deeper into the mountain instead of finding our way out of it. I didn't like it.

Another thing I didn't like – it was getting cold. *Really* cold. It was only when I tried to call to Aaron and my teeth were chattering so much I could hardly move my mouth that I realised *quite* how cold it was.

Finally, I called out to him. 'A-Aaron!'

He stopped and turned. Behind the glowing light

of my crystal, his face was white as ice. 'What?' he asked. His lips looked blue.

'It's f–f–freezing!' I said.

'I know. I think we definitely need to turn back.'

'I agree.' I held my crystal up and we turned back the way we'd come. Just ahead of us, I noticed something I hadn't seen on the way here. A fork in the tunnel. I didn't know which one we had come from. A prickle of fear that felt like an icy spear ran through my chest.

'It's that way,' Aaron said, pointing down the opposite fork from the one I would have chosen.

'I think it's that way,' I said, pointing down the other one.

The icy spear grew branches and spread out along my arms and legs, filling me with dread. We were lost. Trapped in a cold, damp, dark place inside a mountain covered in a glacier – and no one had the slightest idea we were even here.

Aaron was fumbling in a pocket.

'What are you doing?'

'I'm calling Neptune,' he said. 'He told us to get in touch if we had anything to tell him.'

'He told us to get in touch with information, not to call him if we completely messed up the whole mission and got ourselves lost in the process.'

Aaron stopped rummaging for a moment. Then he brightened, and began groping around in his pocket again. 'Mr Beeston, then,' he said. 'He *definitely* told us to call if we got into trouble. He'll help us.'

I didn't want to dampen Aaron's enthusiasm by telling him I could probably count the number of times Mr Beeston had been helpful on the fingers of one hand. And, to be fair, I didn't have any better ideas.

'Where is it?' Aaron mumbled. 'I had it. I'm sure I brought it with me. I must have done.'

'You've lost your shell phone?'

'It looks like it,' he said hopelessly. 'I must have dropped it somewhere.'

The tiny moment of optimism fell away, just like the drops of water had earlier – out of reach and dispersing into nothingness. 'Brilliant!'

Aaron glared at me. 'Well, at least I didn't give it away before we even got here!' he snapped.

A moment later, he took a step towards me. 'Emily, I'm sorry,' he said.

'No, you're right. It was a stupid thing to do.'

'Look, it doesn't matter. There's nothing we can do about it. We'll just have to keep trying different routes till we find our way out of here – which we will do. OK?'

'Mmm,' I mumbled.

Aaron lifted my chin. 'OK?' he repeated more firmly.

'OK,' I agreed.

'Right. You pick,' he said. 'Which one?'

I pointed half-heartedly down the tunnel I'd thought we'd taken to get here. 'Let's try this one first.'

'OK, here's what we're going to do,' Aaron said, taking charge and making me want to kiss him for about the twentieth time since we'd agreed how great it was to be friends. 'We give it a hundred paces, and if nothing looks familiar by then, we turn back and try the other one.'

It was about as good a plan as we were likely to make, so I agreed, and we set off into the darkness once again.

Eighty-four, eighty-five, eighty-six . . . I counted to myself as we walked, almost positive we were going in the wrong direction and about to say so, when we turned a corner and saw something just ahead. It looked like a sculpture. A house made of ice.

Aaron must have seen it at the same moment, as he stopped in his tracks. 'What the—'

'It looks like a guard's hut or something,' I said. It had a pointed top, three solid walls, and the third had an arched opening.

Aaron was saying something, but I didn't hear it. I was looking beyond the ice house – at a scene I had no words to describe.

'Aaron,' I whispered.

There were sculptures *everywhere*. Ice tables, ice pillars, ice chandeliers, even ice people – or ice heads anyway. We couldn't see their bodies from where we were.

It was as though a whole team of ice sculptors had lived here for years, working non-stop before disappearing and leaving nothing but their work behind. Maybe that was *exactly* what had happened. I certainly couldn't think of any other explanation.

Aaron let out a low, whistling breath. 'Wow!'

I took two more steps and looked down at the statues again. That was when I realised something else.

'The statues!' I said, my voice shaking as much as my knees.

Aaron glanced down in the direction I was pointing. 'But they're . . .'

I looked at him. 'I know,' I said. 'They're merpeople.'

We stared at the mer-statues. They were so realistic. Some of them were sculpted sitting on boulders, others horizontal, tails out, as if swimming through the sea. Their tails were so intricate, their faces so lifelike.

A sheen of some sort seemed to surround them all. 'How on earth have they done that?' I asked.

Aaron pointed towards the top of the sheen. 'Look, it's wavy, just like the surface of the sea.'

It was as though the sculptors had created an entire world of merpeople, complete with the ocean. But why would someone produce such amazing art and keep it hidden in a place like this?

I leaned forward to take a closer look, holding my crystal out in front of me to shed more light on the statues. I was about to take another step when Aaron screamed from behind me.

'Emily! Careful!'

He grabbed the back of my coat, stopping me taking another step. As he grabbed me, the crystal fell from my hand.

'Why did you—' I began. And then I looked down. We were on the edge of a precipice. I hadn't realised.

The crystal was still falling – and if Aaron hadn't grabbed me, I would have gone with it. As I stared, I noticed something else, right in the middle of the display. The largest statue of them all.

'Aaron!' I gulped. 'Look at that!'

He followed my shaking finger. 'But . . . but that's . . .'

I felt as though the ice had crept into my throat, my chest, my stomach – it was inside the whole of me. There was no explanation for what we were looking at, none at all.

Down below us, sculpted in the finest detail you could imagine, and more lifelike than anything I had ever seen, was Neptune.

Chapter Ten

We stood, transfixed, staring at the Neptune sculpture and at the crystal, which was still glowing and had landed on the hazy sheen below.

'Emily, this is creeping me out,' Aaron said in a whisper.

'I agree. Let's get out of here.'

We turned to head back the way we'd come – but before we'd taken more than two steps, something stopped us in our tracks. It was a creaking noise, a bit like the sound we'd heard at the top of the hole when the ice had begun to melt – only this was about a hundred times louder. It was coming from down below.

I looked back. The sheen was beginning to dissolve in the exact spot where the crystal had landed. The crystal was burning a hole through the shimmering 'sea', carving a well that was growing deeper and wider by the second, glowing and sparkling as it drilled into the ice. As the well grew, something strange started happening to the statues within it. The ones nearest to the crystal began to thaw!

'What's going on?' Aaron's voice had an edge of panic I'd never heard before.

'I have no idea,' I said. Part of me wanted to run away, wanted to get the heck out of there as fast as I possibly could, wanted to turn back the clock and never let Neptune talk us into this crazy mission in the first place. But another part of me couldn't move. I couldn't take my eyes away from what was happening.

Bit by bit, the sheen was turning into water. Shapes that had been beautifully sculpted merpeople only minutes earlier began to writhe and stretch and swish their tails. Sculpted fish came to life and began swimming in the well of water opening up around them.

Soon, the well had spread into something very similar to the shape of the crystal itself. A giant, jagged droplet of space in the ice, big enough for about six or seven merpeople and countless fish to start swimming in.

The melting seemed to have stopped. Around the crystal-shaped well, everything else was still ice, apart from tiny, watery splinters. Inside it, the scene was very different. Merpeople swam towards each other, hugged, shook hands, smiled and laughed. The fish swam frantically around, forming shoals to explore their new giant fishbowl together.

And then I saw something right at the edge of the melted bowl. It looked like a small shark. It was swimming upwards through one of the splinters in the ice – heading in our direction. Not only that, but it had some kind of weapon with it. It looked like it was carrying a long spear in its mouth.

'Aaron, what's that?' I gasped.

'I've got no idea – but I think it's seen us.'

He was right. The shark was heading straight for us – and it didn't look friendly. Nor did the spear that I could now see was at least as long as its body.

'Let's go!' Aaron yelped.

I didn't need telling twice. In fact, I didn't even need telling once. I was already running out of that creepy place as fast as my shaking, slipping legs would carry me.

I don't know how we did it. Maybe terror is good for improving your sense of direction. But we ran and ran, hurling ourselves along rocky tracks, pelting down forks in the tunnels without even thinking until, eventually, the tunnel began to feel like the one we'd come down in the first place.

A tiny glow of light began to emerge ahead of us. We'd done it! We'd found our way out!

Except, once we were outside the mountain, nothing looked familiar. This wasn't where we'd come in. We came in underwater. This entrance had water lapping at the rocks, but not deep enough to swim in.

We waded through the water until it grew deeper. Then we threw ourselves in and let our tails form. We swam close to the surface, looking around for something familiar. The fjord opened up to a wider stretch of sea. Over the other side, there was a port with buildings and ships.

'Emily, look over there,' Aaron said, pointing at the port. I squinted into the sun – which was dazzling my eyes even though it was the middle of the night! And then I noticed it. A ship. *Our* ship! 'Please tell me that isn't a mirage,' I said.

Aaron smiled. 'I remember now. In the brochure, it said there was a midnight concert on tonight, at a town on the other side of the glacier.'

'We've been all the way through the mountain range and come out on the other side?'

Aaron shrugged. 'It's the only thing that makes sense. We'll need to hurry, though. The programme said the ship was sailing again at two.' He glanced at his watch. 'It's half past one. We've got thirty minutes.'

We swam harder than I'd ever swum in my life. Finally, we pulled ourselves out of the water in a rocky inlet, just out of sight of the boat, and waited for what felt like for ever for our legs to re-form. Then we ran like mad and reached the ship, panting and breathless, just as they were about to start lifting the gangplank.

'Got in by the skin of your teeth there,' the steward said with a smile as we showed our passenger cards and stepped inside. 'Had fun?'

'Mm,' I said, not even bothering to try to sound convincing.

As the large doors slid closed behind us and the ropes were thrown up to the ship from the men on the quay, I could have cried with relief.

'We made it,' Aaron said. He put his arms around me, and this time, I didn't try to stop him.

'There you are!' Mr Beeston's voice made me leap out of my skin – and out of Aaron's arms. 'I've been looking for you all night. Pacing corridors, searching the coastline, coming back here every ten minutes.'

He stopped and looked properly at us. I imagine the combination of grime and gravel, messed up hair, torn clothes and a hundred different emotions on our faces probably didn't make for the most attractive sight.

'I'm forgetting myself – forgive me,' Mr Beeston mumbled. 'I've just been so concerned. Are you all right, the pair of you?'

Aaron nodded.

'Just about,' I said.

Mr Beeston fiddled with a loose strand of hair, flattening it over his head. As I looked at him, I realised he looked exhausted. It was only then that it hit me: it was the middle of the night. Suddenly, I was so tired I wasn't even hungry any more. I just needed sleep.

'I have to get to bed,' I said.

'Of course, of course!' Mr Beeston said hurriedly. 'We can catch up in the morning.'

We made our way to the corridor. Aaron and Mr Beeston's cabin was in one direction; mine was in the other.

'Millie knows nothing of this,' Mr Beeston said as we walked. 'I told her you were spending the evening with a family who had children your age.'

'All this time?' I glanced at a clock on the wall. It was twenty past two. Mr Beeston waved a hand as if to shake my question off. 'Different rules apply when it is daylight for twenty-four hours,' he said. 'Anyway, I went past your cabin earlier and you could hear her snores from outside the door. I don't think she will even notice you come in.'

I stared at Mr Beeston. I still couldn't get used to the idea that the man who had spent the first twelve years of my life spying on me was now our greatest ally. 'Thank you,' I said simply.

He fiddled with a button on his jacket. 'Go on, get to bed,' he said softly.

We parted company and I headed back to my cabin. I gently opened the door. Mr Beeston had been right. Millie was lying flat on her back, arms spread out, mouth wide open, snoring like a horse.

At any other time, the sound might have bothered me. But after everything we'd just been through, *nothing* was going to keep me awake.

Five minutes later, I was in my bed, fast asleep, and for all I knew, snoring just as loudly as Millie.

I dreamt I was swimming in the roughest sea I'd ever known. Up, down, thrown all around. Wave after wave kept washing over me, pulling me down into the belly of the ocean and then spitting me out again.

A sudden lurch to the side woke me with a start. I opened my eyes and looked round. *Just a dream.*

Millie was already up. She was sitting on the end of her bed peering into the mirror as she put her eye make-up on. 'Morning,' she said with a smile. 'Bit early for you, isn't it?'

I looked at the clock. Six thirty! I was about to say something when the boat dipped and Millie fell sideways.

'Bit rough out there this morning,' she said, putting her lipstick away.

Lying down wasn't feeling very pleasant any more. I dragged myself out of bed and rubbed my eyes. The boat dipped again, this time taking a bit of my stomach with it.

'Millie,' I said. 'I need to go outside.'

We got dressed and went up to the roof deck. There were a few people already out there. They obviously weren't so keen on this morning's swell, either.

I looked around. 'Hey, look!' I pointed to the back of the boat. Aaron and Mr Beeston were standing separate from the others, gripping the handrail and talking close together. We made our way over to join them.

Things took a turn for the worse as we crossed the deck. The ship suddenly seemed to rise almost vertically on a massive wave. Then it careered down the other side, as if we were on a rollercoaster ride.

We made it to the back just in time to grip the railings.

Aaron and Mr Beeston stumbled over to join us. Looking out at the horizon, it seemed the ocean had erupted. The sea was like a mountain range, rising and falling with enormous peaks and troughs. White froth foamed angrily over the top of every peak.

I turned to Mr Beeston. 'What's going on?'

'I have no idea,' he said sombrely. 'Usually, a storm like this means only one thing.'

He didn't even have to say the word. I knew what he meant. This had to have something to do with Neptune.

'But why?' Aaron asked, following on from my thoughts as though I'd spoken them out loud.

I thought back over the events of the night. What did any of it mean? Had we got the whole thing wrong? Was Neptune angry?

Ding dong ding! 'Ladies and gentlemen, we are experiencing some heavy weather,' a voice crackled over the loudspeaker. 'We advise all passengers to return to their cabins until further notice. We shall be turning the ship around and returning to our last port, so that we can find a safe harbour until this weather passes. I repeat, please return to your cabins immediately and remain there until we dock in approximately one hour. Thank you and we apologise for any inconvenience.'

We inched our way to the door, and waited behind the other passengers to go in. Millie went first, then Mr Beeston, then Aaron. I was about to follow them when something caught my eye. Something in the sea.

Millie was holding the door open for me.

'I've just got something caught in my shoe. Need to sort it. I'm right behind you.'

'I'll wait,' Millie said, swaying as she held the door.

'No, you go,' I said. 'I'll only be a second.'

'OK, but be quick,' she said. 'I don't want you out here while it's like this.'

As Millie let the door close, I looked around to make sure no one was watching, then I carefully picked my way to the side of the boat. I stared so hard at the peaks and troughs of the swell that my eyes began to water. Had I imagined it?

I was about to leave when I saw it again. A tail! Flashing up in the water before disappearing again. What was it? A shark? A whale?

Come on, come on, I whispered, desperate to find out what it was before one of the ship's officials came out and ordered me back to my cabin.

And then I saw it again. It was closer this time. And it was familiar. And even though I had no idea how in the world I could possibly be right, I knew *exactly* who that tail belonged to.

Shona!

Suddenly, she poked her head above the water,

and waved an arm at me. Then she pointed to the harbour we were heading for.

'See you there?' I called.

Shona nodded, and with a flick of her tail dived back under the water.

I went inside to join the others, my mind spinning with confusion – and with excitement. My best friend was here!

The excitement was tempered only by one fearful question.

Why?

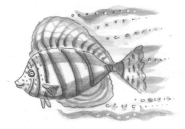

Chapter Eleven

$\mathcal{T}$he moment the ship docked in the port, I was in the water. I didn't even wait for the doors to open. I hung around at the back of the ship on level three, the lowest one with an outside deck. I looked around, making sure there was no one about. And then, as gracefully and silently as I could, I dived into the choppy water.

She was there in moments.

'Shona!'

'Emily!'

We fell into each other's arms. 'You are real, aren't you?' I gasped. 'It's not a dream?'

'It's not a dream,' Shona said seriously. 'But when I've told you why I'm here, you might wish it was.'

Despite Neptune's potion on my body, I turned cold inside. 'What is it? Why *are* you here? How did you get here? How did you know where we were?'

Shona held up a hand. 'Whoah! One thing at a time.'

I took a breath. 'OK. How did you get here?'

'It wasn't the easiest thing in the world,' she admitted. 'I swam some of it, and caught a few lifts.'

'Lifts?' I gasped. 'Who with?'

'A couple of dolphins to begin with. They were great. Then I had to swim a bit more. That bit was quite tough as the currents weren't going my way. Luckily a lovely blue whale spotted me and helped me out. Then finally, a pod of orcas brought me the last couple of hundred miles.'

I stared at Shona. I literally didn't know what to say. She had done all this – for me? She'd either missed me *really* badly, or something was very, very wrong.

'Do your parents know you're here?' I asked.

Shona blushed. 'They don't know about your trip or anything, so I told them I was going to stay with you on *Fortuna* for a few days. I hate lying to them, but it was important.'

'How did you know where we were?' I asked.

Even if I'd had a hundred guesses as to what her answer might be, I would still never have got it right.

'Neptune told me,' she said.

Before I could do anything more than let my jaw drop open, she went on. 'Well, he didn't actually tell *me*. At least, he didn't *mean* to tell me.'

'Shona, my head is spinning enough without riddles. What's going on? What are you talking about?'

Shona held out the shell phone I'd given her. 'I kept it on me the whole time. Even when I went to bed, I had it beside me on my pillow. And then something woke me up just after I'd gone to bed last night. It sounded like waves crashing over a pebbly beach – and it looked like stars glinting and shining. But it was the shell phone calling.'

'Neptune – trying to get in touch with us.'

Shona nodded. 'I picked up the shell, and straight away I heard him speaking. I couldn't make sense of it at first – it was like he was just shouting random words down the phone.'

That sounded familiar. I still had many of Neptune's early morning ramblings bouncing around in my head. 'What kind of things did he say?'

'I can't remember it all. Most of it didn't make sense. But there were a couple of things he kept repeating over and over.'

'What were they?'

'He said he'd remembered something really important. More important than anything else he'd remembered up to now.'

'Go on,' I said, half desperate to know what it was and half hoping she was going to spin round in a double backflip, splash me with her tail and tell me the entire thing was a big joke and she'd come to take me home.

What she actually said made my *insides* do the double backflip.

'He said he'd remembered he has a brother. A twin, in fact.'

'A *what*?' Neptune had a twin brother? And he'd *forgotten*? Had Shona heard correctly? Surely she must have made a mistake.

'He said all he knew was that he had a long forgotten twin, and that with the return of this memory came a new feeling of dread. Something terrible had happened. Something so terrible that it was still locked behind the doors of his deepest memory.'

Before I could answer, a splashing sound behind me made me spin round.

'Emily!' It was Aaron.

'Where did you come from?' I asked.

'I was looking for you when we docked. I saw you on the deck, and then I saw a couple walking towards you. I could tell you were thinking about jumping into the sea. And they were about to see you do it. I got the feeling that a couple of people setting off a "girl overboard" alarm might not have been part of your plans, so I quickly pointed out a mountain on the other side of the ship and stood chatting with them till I was pretty sure you'd had long enough to do whatever it was you were doing.'

'And then you came down to find me and see what I was up to,' I said.

'I came down to check you were all right,' Aaron corrected me.

'Aww, you two,' Shona said. 'Just as mushy as ever, eh?'

'Hmm,' I said awkwardly.

Aaron's cheeks flushed. He turned to Shona. 'Anyway – what are you doing here? What's happened?'

Shona caught Aaron up on everything she'd told me.

'So then what?' Aaron asked. 'What else did Neptune tell you?'

'Not a lot,' Shona said. 'He spent about five minutes barking down the phone before I had a chance to say anything. Then he suddenly stopped. I wondered if the connection had broken or something, but I couldn't say anything . . .'

'Because then he'd realise it wasn't either of us on the end of the shell phone,' I put in.

'Exactly. He kept saying your names, asking if you could hear him. I was tempted to answer and pretend I was you, but I didn't dare. I couldn't risk getting you into trouble. But he was getting more and more worked up. I've never heard him like that. He kept repeating the thing about his twin brother, and how upset he was, and how bad it was for you. And something about the ice, and a glacier slowly melting, but I couldn't tell what he was saying by then – it was all too garbled.'

'What did you do?' Aaron asked.

'I just held my breath and kept listening. Eventually, when no one was replying, he gave up and went. He said he'd keep trying to remember, and that you had to keep your shell phone nearby and wait for another update.'

'Which we would never get because you had Emily's phone,' Aaron said.

'And you lost yours,' I reminded him sharply.

Shona gave me a questioning look but let it go. 'I guessed something like that must have happened,' she said. 'I tried to call you but nobody answered. That was when I knew I had to come and see you. '

'How did you find us?'

Shona smiled. 'Hanging round with you for the last year has helped me hone my detective skills!' she said. 'Neptune said something about the Land of the Midnight Sun on the shell phone. I looked into it at school. Once I knew where it was, I checked out departure dates of all the ships in the area and found the one that matched up with when you'd left. Then I memorised its itinerary so I knew where you'd be on which day – and here I am!'

I stared at her. 'You did all that for me?' I asked.

'You're my best friend. You'd do the same for me,' Shona said. Then she paused, and reddened. 'Em, I've got something else to tell you . . .'

'What?'

'I was in such a hurry to get to you, I left the shell phone at home. I'm so sorry.'

'It doesn't matter,' I reassured her. 'We've got this far without them; we can manage to carry on without them too.'

We fell silent for a moment as we all tried to figure out exactly *how* to carry on, and what our next step should be. I thought over everything Shona had just told us. And then it hit me. I turned to Aaron. 'The ice statue in the mountain!'

'The one of Neptune?' Aaron said.

I shook my head. 'It wasn't Neptune!'

'It wasn't Neptune? Of *course* it was Neptune. It was . . .' Aaron stopped. I could tell by the way his face drained of colour that he had caught up with my thinking.

'You're right, it wasn't,' he said. 'The ice statue was Neptune's twin brother.'

We filled Shona in on everything we knew and all that had happened. It seemed a bit pointless to hold on to it being a secret now she was actually here with us.

'You have to go back there,' Shona said.

'Back there?' I repeated, hoping I'd heard wrong. I couldn't think of anything in the world I'd like to do less than go back inside that mountain.

'Shona's right,' Aaron said. 'We have to go back to the statue. Neptune's remembered he's got a twin brother, and he's filled with feelings of dread.'

'And he remembers something about ice,' Shona added.

'Neptune's brother is pretty much an ice sculpture, like everything else down there,' I said. 'That must be why Neptune's so upset. Someone turned his brother to ice – and then took his memory away.'

'Exactly,' said Aaron. 'And our mission is to undo what happened.'

'So we have to bring Neptune's brother back to life, and find out who did it – and who stole Neptune's memory,' I said, wishing it wasn't true.

'I wish it wasn't the case either,' Aaron said, reading my mind as usual. I used to find it romantic; now it was just irritating. 'But we have to do it. We finally know exactly what our mission is.'

I nodded. 'We need to take the other crystals – the ones that melted the sculptures. Find Neptune's brother again, and get a crystal to melt him.'

I could hardly believe it, but I knew it was true. We really *did* have to go back to that place. The place where the frozen people were all coming to life and where the scary shark with the giant spear was on the search for us.

I looked out to sea, trying to imagine going out there again. That was when I spotted the swell coming into the harbour. The water had been relatively calm since we'd got in here, but a small hill was rolling towards us now.

'Aaron, Shona . . .' I said, holding out a shaky finger.

They turned to look where I was pointing. Just as they did, the swell hit the outside of the harbour, crashing over the pier as if a bomb had exploded in the water. It was the biggest wave we'd seen yet.

'It's fine,' Shona said calmly. 'We're merfolk. We can handle the swell of the sea.'

'Maybe out in the open ocean we can,' I said. 'But I'm not so sure about a freak wave that seems to be heading directly for us – and is about to fling us against the harbour wall!'

Shona looked again at the wave. She turned pale. 'You're right,' she said.

The swell was rolling higher and higher, building into a peak, and starting to crumble in an avalanche of ferocious white froth.

'We haven't got time to get out of the port!' Aaron gasped.

'Dive down as far as you can!' I yelled over the thundering sound of the wave. 'It'll be gone in a second. If we get separated, meet at—'

And then it came. The wave picked me up like a giant tucking me under its arm. Briefly it lifted me, then *CRASH*, hurled me under. It felt as though the weight of the entire sea was collapsing on top of me, holding me down, then spinning me round and round. Now I knew how it felt to be inside a washing machine on the spin cycle. And I didn't like it.

The world had turned white and silent, and upside down.

I tried to relax and let the water do what it wanted to do. It was only water. It wouldn't hurt me.

Finally, the wave passed and I began to swim back to the surface. Only I wasn't sure which way the surface was. And before I'd got anywhere, the next wave was on me. Thundering over me, wrapping me into a ball and hurling me around.

Again, I tried to stay calm; again I clawed my way towards the light. Again, I was beaten back down.

Finally, after one last pummelling and a couple more dunkings, it was over. The swell had passed.

Gasping and shaking, I looked round. The water was full of bubbles and foam; it looked like the fizziest drink in the world had been shaken up and poured all around me. A hundred tiny silver fish darted towards each other to re-form as a shoal, then turned and swam off as one. A sleepy ray flicked its cape as if to shrug off the swell, and smoothly slithered past. The seabed itself swirled like an underwater sandstorm.

'Emily!' Shona was swimming towards me.

'You OK?' I asked.

'It's Aaron,' she said. 'Come, quick.'

I followed her through the swirling water down to the seabed. Aaron was in the middle of some rocks. Literally.

I swam over to him. He was lying on the sea floor, a huge boulder half on top of his tail, cuts all across his face and arms. 'You're bleeding! What happened?'

Aaron nodded towards the boulder. 'Came out of nowhere,' he said, gasping and wincing as he spoke. 'Wave threw it at me.'

I wanted to swim straight into his arms, kiss him better, tell him I'd do anything I could to stop him from hurting, but I made myself hold back. Instead,

I swam towards the boulder. 'Shona, help me. Let's see if we can move it.'

We pushed and heaved at the boulder as Aaron gripped onto his tail and clenched his teeth against the pain.

'Does it hurt really badly?' I asked.

He just nodded, and tightened his jaw.

'Right, hold on. We'll get it this time,' I said firmly. 'Shona, wait till I say.' I felt for the movement of the swell. If we got the rhythm right, we could do it. 'OK, one, two, three – push!'

We heaved our weight against the boulder. Nothing. 'And again,' I said, as the swell rocked back towards us. 'Push!' Again and again, we heaved and rocked until, finally, the boulder moved enough for Aaron to roll out from under it.

He inched away from the rocks, pulling himself along with his hands. 'I can't use it,' he said. 'My tail – it's not working. I think it's broken.'

'Tails don't break,' Shona said. 'It'll just be bruised.' She glanced at Aaron's tail. It had turned black and purple where the boulder had been on it. 'Badly bruised,' she added.

Aaron tried to move again. 'Aarrgh!' He clutched his tail.

'Try just using the end of it,' I said, 'where it's not so bad.'

Aaron flicked the tip of his tail. It lifted him a tiny bit in the water. 'OK,' he said. 'I can do that.'

Grimacing and white as ice, he inched along at the pace of a starfish.

After about ten minutes, we finally got back to where the ship was moored. 'I can't do this,' Aaron confessed. 'There's no way I can go back to the mountain. I'll just be a liability. You need to go without me. I'm so sorry.'

'Aaron, it's not your fault,' I said softly. Looking at his face creased up with pain and his lifeless, bruised tail dragging along behind him, I couldn't hold on to any of the anger I'd been feeling.

'Let's get Aaron back on the ship, and then I'll go to the mountain with you,' Shona said.

I looked at her. 'Are you sure?'

'Of course I'm sure,' she said. 'No discussion.'

I turned back to Aaron. 'Right, let's go.'

Between us, we got Aaron to the shore and let him rest for a moment. 'You need to go,' he said. 'I'll find Mr Beeston. He'll look after me. I'll be fine. Go on, go. Let's get this thing over.'

'OK.' I briefly touched his hand.

Instantly, he closed his fingers around mine. 'Be careful,' he said. 'I don't want anything to happen to you.'

I felt as if I'd swallowed one of the rocks. It was jamming up my throat. I couldn't speak. Instead, I quickly squeezed his hand before letting go. ' Come on,' I said to Shona. 'Let's go.'

Silently, we swam away from Aaron, away from

the ship, away from the harbour and back to face the mountain, the ice, the spear-wielding shark – and whatever else might have come back to life and be lying in wait for our return.

Chapter Twelve

After swimming for what felt like hours, we
eventually found our way to the mountain.
The first stroke of luck we had was that the tide
had come in, and the entrance Aaron and I had
come out of earlier was underwater now – which
meant Shona could swim into it. I hoped this was a
good omen, and that everything else would go our
way. Hoped, but didn't seriously believe.

After a few twists and turns, and a couple of
changes in direction, Shona stopped swimming.
'Are you sure this is right?' she asked. 'We don't

seem to be getting very far. In fact,' she looked round, 'I think we might be swimming in circles.'

'I think it should be down this way,' I said, trying to sound as if I knew what I was talking about, when in reality *everything* was looking unfamiliar now. It had been a dry cave last time I'd been here, and now the whole thing was submerged – either from the tide, or from the melting ice, or both.

We swam on. Soon, I noticed bits of ice floating past us. That was when I knew we were going the right way. We weren't just swimming down a river created by the high tide anymore – we were swimming through what had been ice last time we came, but had now melted and spilled out along various forks of the tunnel.

'We're nearly there,' I said. One more corner and we would be at the spot that Aaron and I had reached in the night.

And then I heard voices coming our way.

'Hide!' I shoved Shona into a crevice in the wall and squeezed in beside her.

Two mermen were swimming towards us. Their faces were thin and hard. One had straggly, unkempt grey hair; the other was bald. Their tails were like long, sharp, glinting knives: one jet black, the other a shiny, silvery grey. Both wore matching scowls.

'Yes of course, it's obviously fantastic,' one of them said impatiently as they approached our hiding place, 'but none of it matters without Njord.'

The mermen were swimming right past us. I held my breath and prayed they wouldn't see us.

'I know,' the other one replied. Neither of them looked our way. 'We need to find more crystals. One was never going to be enough for him.'

'It would help if we knew where the first one had come from,' the first merman said, and I didn't hear any more of their conversation, as they'd gone out of earshot.

I let out a heavy breath. Clearly too heavy, as one of them turned round.

'What was that?' he said. 'Is someone there?'

'Look! A couple of mermaids in the shadows!' the other one said.

'What do we do?' Shona hissed.

'Swim!'

We flicked our tails as hard as we could, propelling ourselves along the channel, past fish with bright blue bodies and startled looks on their faces and away from the scary-looking mermen.

'Oi! Come back!' the mermen yelled. It took them about half a minute to catch us up. One of them grabbed the end of my tail.

'Who are you?' he demanded. I struggled to get away from him, but he was too strong.

The other one had hold of Shona. 'How did you get here?'

'Let us go!' Shona squealed.

'Let's take them to the boss,' one of the mermen said.

'Are you sure?' the other one replied. 'There's not a lot he can do while he's rooted to the spot.'

'He's not rooted to the spot. He can move his mouth, his fingertips and the tip of his tail; most importantly, he can speak. That's all he needs to do. We follow the great Njord's orders, not our own.'

'What's a "great Njord"?' I asked before I could stop myself. Maybe it was similar to a fjord. It *sounded* similar enough.

'Who, not what!' the merman still gripping my tail with his hands snapped.

'OK, *who's* a Njord, then?'

'Our leader.'

The merman who had hold of Shona nudged his head in the direction we'd been heading. 'Come on,' he said. 'Let's go. They'll find out soon enough.'

Then he leaned down and grabbed a long strand of seaweed. Pulling it up and biting into it with his teeth, he quickly wrapped it a couple of times round the end of Shona's tail. He passed it back to the other merman who did the same to mine.

'Just in case you had other plans,' he said, showing half a mouthful of yellow teeth as he laughed in my face. His breath nearly made me faint. It smelt like a bin full of dead fish that had been left to rot for a year.

The mermen swam along the tunnel, pulling us

behind them. 'Not a bad catch for the first day back in business,' one of them said.

'Instant promotion, I'm thinking,' the other one replied.

Shona and I wriggled and writhed and grimaced as we half swam and half got dragged to the arena in the middle of the mountain. I tried not to think too hard about what was waiting for us, and what this Njord guy was going to do with us once we got there.

'Bring them closer. Let me see their faces!'

The guards had brought us to the exact place we needed to be, to the exact person we had wanted to find: Neptune's brother! I didn't know whether to be terrified or relieved. Although I have to say that after being dragged along and tied up with seaweed, to face an almost identical replica of Neptune – only mostly made out of ice and looking down at me with loathing and disgust on his face – I was tending towards the 'terrified' option.

The water ended in front of Njord so we couldn't swim right up to him. The mermen pulled us as close as we could get.

Before any of them could say anything, I decided to take the initiative. After all, we had come here to help Njord. As soon as he heard that, he was bound to let us go.

I was about to speak. I looked at his face – the only part of him that seemed capable of movement. As I did, it broke into what I guessed was probably meant to be a smile. If you try to imagine a shark as it spots fresh prey and opens its mouth ready to swallow it whole, you'd be halfway to imagining what his smile looked like.

'I am glad you decided to join us,' Njord said as I stared. His voice felt like a snake, slithering around the caves.

'I . . . I . . .' I tried to tell him why we were there, but couldn't find my voice. Instead, I reached a hand into my coat pocket to show him the crystals.

'Silence!' Njord bellowed. For the first time, I seriously began to doubt our plan. Could this really be Neptune's beloved brother? Could Neptune really want us to free him? It didn't seem possible.

The guard roughly grabbed my arm. 'Quiet, you,' he growled, in case I hadn't understood what 'silence' meant. I gripped the crystals even tighter inside my pocket.

Njord stared at me. 'I saw what happened,' he said. 'And I saw that it was an accident. I might have been ice, but my eyes were open. Inside, I was alive. I saw what you had, but it wasn't enough. Yes, it freed my head enough that I can now speak. It freed my fingertips enough that I can now grasp. It freed the tip of my tail enough that I can now flick it with rage and cause a storm.'

Of course! If this was Neptune's twin brother, he probably had the same powers. It was *his* anger that had caused all the freak storms at sea!

'But clearly I need more than one crystal to free me completely,' Njord said, his voice a whisper, so quiet and so sharp and so cold it felt like a thin blade slicing through me. 'And I believe you have it.'

Njord continued to stare at me. My fingertips were warm against the crystals in my pocket, but they didn't seem to want to let go of them. What should I do? I decided the truth was the only strategy that would protect us. After all, we had originally come here to do the very thing he was now asking of us. If only I could get rid of the feeling in my gut screaming at me not to do it.

I spoke quickly. 'We know that someone did this to you,' I said. 'We know who you are. I mean, we think we kind of know your . . . brother?'

Njord raised an eyebrow. 'Continue,' he said.

'Neptune can't remember what happened,' I went on quickly. 'He knows something bad happened to you, and he knows that whoever did it took his memory away. We've come to help you. We want to reunite you with your brother.'

The caves fell silent. Not the tiniest sound. Njord's eyes bored into me. Behind me, Shona and the guards waited for a response. It felt as though the moment itself had frozen.

And then, suddenly, everything changed.

Njord smiled broadly. 'The child has come to help us!' he announced. 'To reunite me with my beloved brother!' Njord laughed a raw, rasping laugh.

He shifted his eyes to look at one of the guards. Njord's neck was still frozen so he couldn't actually move his head. 'Release them both!' he ordered. 'We are all friends!'

The two mermen instantly untied us, bowing low as they backed away again.

Njord smiled at me. 'I'm sorry about that,' he said sweetly. 'I'm sure you can understand we have to take precautions until we know if our visitors are friends or foes.'

I rubbed my tail where it had been tied. 'It's OK,' I said. He had a point. And he *was* Neptune's twin brother, after all. Neptune had never been known for his great social skills. I mean, look how he'd brought Aaron and me to see him at the start of the mission – blindfolded and bundled into fishing nets!

'So, you were saying,' Njord said, his voice oozing friendliness and warmth, 'about wanting to help.'

'We want to bring you and Neptune back together,' I said. 'It's what we were sent here to do.'

'How wonderful,' Njord replied, smiling broadly.

I edged closer to him, wondering exactly what

I was meant to do. Did I have to drop a crystal on him or what? I still had the crystals in my hand, still had my hand in my pocket. I wanted to open my fingers – I really did – but something was stopping me. Fear? Doubt?

Whatever it was, Njord could obviously see it too, as he carried on talking in a soothing, cajoling voice. 'I will be so happy to see my dear brother,' he said. 'So happy to make friends again after such a silly squabble.'

'Squabble?' I asked.

'Oh, we were always at it. It was nothing unusual. A petty disagreement. A bit of silly nonsense that went too far,' Njord looked down at himself, 'and ended up with this.'

'Your disagreement ended up with you being frozen? But how?'

'Oh, you know what brothers are like when they fall out. And when the brothers in question have as much magic and power at their disposal as the likes of us, it can be a bit dramatic when things get out of hand.'

'I understand,' I said, trying to sound as if it were exactly the kind of thing I came across every day: falling out with someone and accidentally finding one of you had been turned to ice. Again, the doubt gripped me. I turned to Shona. She seemed to shake her head. Did she feel the same way as I did?

I closed my fingers more tightly around the crystals. Shona swam to my side. 'Something isn't right,' she whispered, echoing my feelings perfectly.

'I agree,' I whispered back. 'But I don't know what to do about it.'

'Me neither.'

I gathered all the courage I had, and turned to Njord. 'I think you're lying,' I said, imagining myself being carried away by those guards and fed to the shark with the spear.

'We thought someone horrible had done this to you,' Shona said. 'We thought someone turned you to ice and then took Neptune's memory away so he couldn't help you.'

'And your point?' Njord replied.

'Our point,' I said, 'is that we don't understand why Neptune would be so desperate to free you again if *he* was the one who turned you to ice in the first place! He told us something awful had happened, and we assumed he meant something awful had happened to *you*.'

'But if Neptune himself did it,' Shona continued, 'how can we be sure he really wants you to be unfrozen?'

'We just can't take that risk,' I told him.

Njord frowned. 'My dear brother has clearly come to regret his actions,' he said.

'Hmm,' I murmured.

'Look, it was a silly brothers' prank that got out

of hand – no harm done. Now, let's just get on with unfreezing the rest of me and we can all have a lovely reunion.' A tight edge had crept into Njord's voice.

I looked at Shona. 'I'm not convinced,' I said.

She shook her head. 'Nor am I.'

Njord fixed his steely eyes on me. 'There is nothing not to be convinced about,' he hissed. 'Now give me the crystals!'

I flicked my tail and folded my arms and tightened my grip on the crystals.

Njord sucked on his teeth. 'Neptune wronged me,' he hissed. 'I had something he wanted, and he wasn't happy, all right? And yes, *he* did this to me. He did it out of *greed*, the only thing that truly motivates him!'

I turned to Shona. 'To be fair, that does sound quite typical of Neptune.'

Njord's face was red, his cheek pulsing as he spoke through gritted teeth. 'He probably remembers how he wronged me and wants to make amends. And he probably sent you because he knows you can undo the damage.'

Shona and I looked at each other. 'I don't know what to do,' I whispered.

Njord's fingertips were reaching out to me, edging between the crushed, frozen ice. They were like tendrils of seaweed, stretching and swaying on the tide. 'Please,' he begged. 'Help me. Help my brother. Bring us back together.' A tear edged out of his eye and trickled a wet track down his face.

Maybe he *was* telling the truth. I pushed one of the crystals deeper into my pocket, just in case, and slowly brought the other one out of my pocket. The second I did, Njord's face changed.

'Seize her!' he bellowed.

The guard was by my side in moments. Before I even knew what was happening, he had grabbed my arm and snatched the crystal from my hand.

'Take them away!' Njord ordered. His eyes had narrowed to black slits, his forehead creased like corrugated iron. The other guard had hold of Shona. He quickly tied the seaweed around her waist. A minute later, we were prisoners again.

The guard who had stolen the crystal turned to Njord. 'Now what, my lord?'

'Now, release me from my prison!' Njord bellowed. 'Give me the crystal!'

The guard swam towards Njord and placed the crystal into Njord's outstretched hand. Njord closed his fingers around it. He shut his eyes. 'At last, I will be free,' he said. 'My turn to reign is nearly here.'

'The girls, my lord,' said the guard who held Shona. 'What do you want us to do with them?'

Njord didn't even open his eyes. Smiling to himself, he said, 'Take them to the dungeons. Lock them away while I decide what is to be done with them – and with my traitorous eel of a brother.'

The guards turned and swam off, dragging us along the winding tunnels and down to a dark, cold cave in the deep belly of the mountain.

The guards threw us in a cell and locked the door. Laughing and congratulating themselves, they swam away.

I was beginning to get a sense of déjà vu. Except, this time, I had the feeling Neptune wasn't about to turn up and tell us things weren't how they looked.

I suspected things were *exactly* how they looked. And I can tell you, they didn't look good.

I swam to the edge of the cave and slid down the wall next to a pipe with a brown jellyfish poking out of its end. Beside me, a bunch of thin reeds were tangled up like a plate of spaghetti. They swayed with the movement of the water.

I put my head in my hands and wondered if things could get any worse.

Which was pretty much the moment that they did.

'Emily.' Shona was tugging on my arm. Her voice was as wobbly as the jellyfish on the pipe.

I looked up. 'What?'

She pointed to the bars at the front of the cave. Or, more accurately, she pointed just outside the bars to the tunnel, and to what was swimming along it.

I put everything I possibly had into stopping myself from screaming – mainly because it was such a small space that I would probably have deafened Shona if I had done, and the last thing I needed was for my best friend to be incapable of ever hearing me again.

Actually, that's not quite true. The last thing I needed was to see a shark with a giant spear on the front of its head swimming directly towards us.

But, unfortunately, that was exactly what I'd got.

'Just stay calm,' I said to Shona.

Who was I kidding? *Stay calm?* How were we meant to do *that*?

The shark was coming closer. It was right outside the cage. What if it got in? Had Njord sent it? Was this it? Was this was how it was all going to end? After everything we'd been through, were we going to be a shark's mid-morning snack?

It came closer still. The spear was up against the bars now.

Shona edged towards me and gripped my arm. 'I'm scared,' she said.

'Me too. Just . . . just don't panic,' I said, stating the obvious and the impossible yet again.

We swam slowly and carefully backwards, edging into the furthest corner of the cave.

The shark pressed its head against the bars. Its

spear poked right through them and into our cell. We had nowhere to go. The spear was longer than the cave.

Shaking, and trying to remember the words to any prayer I'd ever heard, I closed my eyes as the spear edged towards me and touched my forehead.

This was it. Game over.

Chapter Thirteen

*D*o not fear me.

What was that? I opened my eyes. The shark and its spear had retreated. It wasn't going to smash my skull in. Not yet, anyway.

'Shona, was that you?'

Shona was curled up next to me, her tail flapping as fast as a butterfly's wings, her eyes tightly closed.

'Was what me?' she asked, nervously opening an eye.

I am not your enemy.

'That!'

Shona stared at me. 'What?'

'The voice. Listen.'

She will not hear me.

OK, this was getting freaky. 'Did you hear that?' I asked, a little less certainly.

Shona sighed. 'Did I hear *what?*' she demanded. 'All I can hear is you asking me questions – and my heart thumping at about a thousand beats per minute.'

'Right,' I said. 'Sorry. I'm just imagining it. Must be the waves, or maybe one of the guards somewhere.'

You are not imagining it. And I am not a guard.

I jumped up, swam to the front of the cave and looked both ways. 'Come on – stop hiding!' I shouted. 'I know there's someone there. You're just trying to freak me out.'

Shona swam to join me. She looked left and right, too. 'There's no one there.'

'Exactly. They're too cowardly to show their faces, hiding in the shadows and calling to us like that.' I stuck my head through the bars. 'Ha! See! Called your bluff there, didn't I? You can't scare me, you know. I'm not—'

Look directly in front of you.

The voice nearly made me leap out of my scales. Look directly in front of me? I wasn't going to do *that*. The only thing right in front of me was the scary shark with the giant spear. Nothing in the world would make me look *that* in the eyes! Unless . . .

I slowly turned my head to face it. 'Is it you?' I whispered.

'Is *what* me?' Shona asked.

'Not you.' I pointed at the shark. I swallowed hard, and then I looked it in the eyes. 'You.'

The shark lowered its head in a soft nod.

Yes, it's me.

OK. So it wasn't enough that we were trapped in a cave, down in the belly of a mountain, in a place no one would ever find us as long as we lived. Now I was going mad as well, hearing sharks talking to me. Well, that was just great.

You brought me back to life. In exchange, I will be your loyal friend for ever.

'What if I don't want a spear-carrying shark to be my friend for ever?' I said.

'What?' Shona asked. 'What are you talking about?'

I am not a shark.

'Not a shark? You certainly look like a shark to me.'

I am a narwhal.

'A what?'

'Emily! What are you talking about? Are you OK?' Shona was shaking my arm.

How was I meant to explain this? Lie? Make something up? Brush it off? No. This was Shona.

She was my best friend, and I'd always told her the truth about everything. I wasn't going to change that now – even if she did decide that I'd lost the plot and was probably better off being locked up, after all.

I nudged a finger at the shark – or the narwhal – whatever that was. 'It's talking to me,' I said.

Shona let out a breath and nodded slowly. 'O . . . K . . .' she said.

'Honestly!' I insisted.

Shona looked at the creature, still hovering outside the cage, still directly facing us.

As she did, I looked more closely at it, too. That was when I realised it didn't actually look like a shark. It didn't have a fin on its back, and actually, apart from the spear, it didn't look frightening.

It looked more like a small whale than a shark. It had a dark black back, two small fins, a little tail and tiny black eyes. Its tummy was speckled with grey spots that looked a bit like freckles, and its spear wasn't all that scary. In fact, it made it look almost magical – like a unicorn of the sea.

'You know, there's something familiar about it, now I think of it,' Shona said. 'I'm sure I've seen a picture of one of these somewhere – at school probably.' She thought for a moment. 'I think it was in Seas and Species. There are these rare creatures that have spears sticking out of their heads. What were they called now?' She scrunched up her forehead, tapping a finger against her mouth and flicking her tail from side to side as she thought.

'Um. Were they called narwhals?' I asked hesitantly.

'Narwhals! That's it!' Shona said, clapping her hands together. 'Wait! How did you know that?'

I pointed at the narwhal. 'The narwhal told me.'

Shona stared at the narwhal, then back at me. 'It *told* you?'

Please, tell your friend I am a "he" not an "it".

'Er, he's a he,' I said awkwardly.

Shona swam up to the bars of the cave. 'Wow. This is, like, one of the rarest creatures in the ocean.'

Stay here.

The narwhal's voice was urgent.

I will be back.

In a flash, he was gone.

'Did we scare him off?' Shona asked.

'I don't know. I don't think so. He said to stay here.' Not that we had any choice in the matter.

'What do you mean "he said"? I didn't hear anything. Are you making this up?'

I thought for a minute. How was I going to get Shona to believe me? Then I remembered something: the kraken. 'Shona, do you remember on Allpoints Island when I could hear the kraken's thoughts?'

'Because you were the one who woke it.'

'Exactly! Maybe this is similar to that. *I* dropped

the crystal that woke the narwhal, so I'm the one who can hear his voice.'

'Wow,' Shona said.

'But I think he only activated it when he touched me with his spear just now.'

Neither of us had time to say anything else as a swishing sound was coming towards us. We both looked up to see the guards heading back to our cell.

'Njord sent us to search you,' one of them said, reaching into his tail pocket for a key. 'Says we need another crystal. He thought two would be enough and they've melted everything else, but because the spell was cast directly on him, it turns out he needs one more. And you're our best hope of finding it.'

Suddenly, another guard appeared from nowhere. He must have been hiding out of sight in the tunnel's dark shadows. 'Yeah, I got that message too,' he said. 'Already searched them.'

The guards looked up at him. 'You got the message?' one of them asked. He eyed the new guard suspiciously. 'We never saw you there.'

The new guard pointed to his ear. It looked as though he had something stuck inside it. An earpiece, maybe a microphone. Was he getting orders directly from Njord? I dreaded to think what instructions he would be given next. 'Perhaps you haven't got one of these,' he said pointedly to the other guards.

They looked at each other. They didn't seem happy.

'I've told you, I've already searched them,' the new guard said, impatiently. 'They've got nothing. If they ever *had* a third crystal, they certainly haven't got it any more.'

'But they've *got* to have one. Njord still isn't free. His neck has melted enough that he can move his head around, his tail is flapping like crazy and his arms have melted too, but his body is still stuck fast. He needs a third crystal. We can't go back without one.'

'In that case, you'd better find it quickly. If they ever had another one, my guess is they dropped it when you were bringing them here. Search the tunnel. I'm sure you'll find it soon and get yourself back in Njord's good books.'

The two guards exchanged a quick look. Then, with a shrug, they turned and swam off. As soon as they had rounded the corner, the new guard came towards us and pulled a chain of keys from around his neck. As he approached the door, I noticed he was younger than he'd sounded. He only looked a couple of years older than us – maybe fourteen or fifteen. He was quite tall and very thin, with deep blue eyes, a shiny green tail and hair so blond it was almost white. Shona was staring at him, and blushing. He glanced at her and allowed himself a brief smile.

'Come on,' he said, rattling a key in the lock. 'We haven't got long. Even a pair of idiots like those two won't take long to figure out I was lying and come back to search you.' He rattled the key a bit more. 'I'm Seth,' he added.

'You were lying?' I asked. 'You didn't get orders directly from Njord?'

Seth pulled the black thing out of his ear and held it out to show us. It was a small pebble! 'What, with this?' he asked, a hint of a smile on his face. 'No, I didn't get my orders directly from Njord.'

'Why are you doing this?' Shona asked, flicking her hair to the side as she spoke. Was she flirting with him? At a time like *this*?

Seth held out a hand to help her out of the cell door. Not that she needed it. She had been swimming perfectly well on her own for her entire life. I swam out behind her and joined them in the tunnel.

'Because of what I saw,' he said. He nodded at me. 'I saw you talking to the narwhal.'

Oh, great. He must have thought I was completely bonkers, swimming around talking to a strange sea creature who didn't show any signs of talking back.

'Hmm,' I said.

Seth looked at me seriously. 'No one can do that,' he whispered. 'No one . . . except Neptune.'

'Neptune?' I blurted out. 'But . . . but . . .'

He glanced around furtively. 'Listen, we haven't got long,' he said. 'I'll tell you all you need to know to keep you safe. And then you have to get out of here as quickly as you can.'

He pulled us into a thin crack in the wall of the tunnel. It must have been where he'd been hiding when the guards had turned up.

'Neptune and Njord used to rule the seas together, many hundreds of years ago,' Seth began, 'but things were never easy between them.'

That didn't surprise me. I knew how changeable Neptune's moods could be – and from what I'd seen, Njord's were just as unpredictable.

'They both had spies. Njord had his in Neptune's camp; Neptune had his in Njord's. The spies would work their way into the highest positions possible, and report back to their real leaders.'

'You're a spy for Neptune!' Shona breathed.

Seth nodded. 'Or, at least, I was – before the big freeze. I've been stuck here, turned to ice and frozen in time, along with everyone and everything else around me for, well, I don't know how long.' He dragged his eyes away from Shona and smiled at me. 'You released us,' he said. 'Your crystal set us free.'

'And the narwhal?' I asked.

'The narwhal was Neptune's special pet. His most treasured, most loyal follower. Only Neptune's powers were strong enough to communicate with him – to do what I just witnessed *you* doing.'

I looked down, embarrassed.

'Which means that either Neptune or the narwhal knows you are to be trusted,' Seth went on. 'In which case, I have no hesitation in putting my trust in you as well.'

'So what now?' I asked.

'We have to get you out of here before the guards come back. I will show you a secret exit. You must take the narwhal with you and keep him safe.'

'How exactly are we meant to do that?' I said.

Seth shook his head. 'You'll have to figure something out. We haven't got time to think about it now. All I know is that you have to get the narwhal back to Neptune. If the narwhal is reunited with Neptune, I believe that Neptune will understand and remember – and come back to us.'

'I don't get it,' Shona said.

'You don't have to – and I haven't got time to explain further. Listen.'

Voices, coming closer. The guards were on their way back. We'd run out of time already!

'Come on.' Seth grabbed Shona's hand and pulled her deeper into the crevice. They disappeared into the darkness and I followed behind. Silently, we swam through the secret hairline crack in the mountain, down and down into the dark, silent depths.

After we'd been swimming for a while, and left

the voices far behind, Seth stopped and turned to face us. 'I have to leave you here.'

My eyes had got a tiny bit used to the darkness and I looked around to see where 'here' actually was. We were still swimming through the crack, but it had now opened up into a round clearing.

Above the clearing, dark rocks formed an arched roof. Below, there was a dark well.

I couldn't see the bottom of it. It looked like the kind of thing you'd dare someone to swim down – if you had a really sick sense of humour. Who would want to swim into a pitch black well that plunged vertically down the middle of a mountain, and was only a tiny bit wider than your own body?

'You have to swim down there,' Seth said, pointing into the well. I might have guessed.

'Many years ago, the bottom of this well was the meeting place for Neptune's spies. There are only a handful of us who know of it. Wait down there for the narwhal. He will come. Once he is with you, follow the tunnel. It will lead you out.'

'What about you?' Shona asked. 'Will you be OK?'

'I'll be fine. I've kept myself safe before; I'll do it again. As long as Njord doesn't receive a third crystal, he won't get free. But now he's melted even more than before, you must be careful. He'll get more and more angry.'

'Which means the sea will get more and more rough?' I asked.

'Exactly. You've felt the storms from his rage already. They will get worse.'

I looked down the dark well, and tried not to think about it. 'Come on,' I said to Shona. 'Let's go.'

'Good luck,' Seth called to us.

'Thanks for everything,' Shona called back.

And then we flipped our bodies over, spun our tails hard, and headed down into the murky depths.

The narwhal was already waiting for us at the bottom of the well.

I'm happy to see you again.

'I'm happy to see you too,' I said, smiling at him and realising I meant it. I looked at his freckled face. How could I have thought he was scary? He was anything but scary. He was . . . cute.

Are you ready?

'We're ready,' I said.

Follow me.

The narwhal swam to the edge of the well. For a moment, nothing happened. And then the wall began to crumble, right around the spot where the spear was touching it. It was as if the narwhal was drilling a hole right through the wall with his spear!

The wall sparked and sparkled, and dust fell into the water all around us. A moment later, the narwhal moved away, to reveal a perfect hole, just big enough for the three of us to swim through.

After you.

I swam into the hole. Shona swam into it behind me. Then the narwhal followed and turned back round again, pointing his spear into the hole. We watched as the sparks flew and fizzed again – and the hole closed up!

'How did he do that with his spear?' Shona asked.

I'm sure the narwhal smiled. I couldn't see it – just kind of felt it happen.

You do not get to be Neptune's most loyal pet without having a few tricks to call on.

'He used Neptune's magic!' I explained.

Oh, and please, it is a tusk, not a spear.

'OK. Sorry.'

Now, let's get out of here.

The secret tunnel on the other side of the hole was much wider than the one we'd been in earlier. And we were finally swimming back up. For the first time in hours, it actually felt as if we might get out of this mountain alive.

We swam and swam until, finally, we saw a tiny light ahead of us.

Spurred on by the hope of getting out, we swam

faster, on and on, until we came to a jagged archway in the rock. Beyond it, the sun fanned its rays across the opening, shining so brightly I had to close my eyes as I swam.

And then we were out. We'd done it. We were back in the blue water of the fjord and the bright, bright light of the sun. I turned to look back at the mountain. Overhead, a large eagle circled its peak. It looked like the one that had swooped down at me when I'd been here with Aaron. Its wings were silhouetted against the sun as it flew around the mountain. It seemed to be looking for something.

I was about to point it out when the vibrations began.

The flat, calm water of the fjord creased into a corrugated mass of lumps and bumps – all heading our way. I guessed the guards had told Njord they couldn't find a third crystal – and this was his response.

'Dive!' Shona yelled.

The three of us darted down under the water, away from the worst of the swell. Even so, it still caught my tail and spun me round in a triple somersault the likes of which I'd never quite managed to pull off on my own.

Come. Climb on. I will take you.

I clambered aboard the narwhal's back and called to Shona. 'Come on. The narwhal says he'll take us back to the ship.'

Shona climbed onto the narwhal's back behind me.

I held on to his tusk and prepared myself for a bumpy ride.

We were back at the ship in a fraction of the time it had taken us to swim to the mountain earlier. Luckily, it was still in the harbour – although as we approached, we heard two loud blasts of the horn, which signalled that it was about to leave.

'We have to hurry,' I said. 'There's usually about five minutes after the horn has sounded.'

'What about me?' Shona asked.

I will take care of her. We will follow the boat. We will never be far from you. Now, go.

'The narwhal will look after you,' I told her.

And with that, I climbed off the narwhal's back, gave Shona a last hug, and swam like crazy to get to the harbour in time to sneak back onto the ship.

'Decided to go for a dip, did you?' The steward at the door asked, laughing as she pointed to my wet hair.

'Hah, ha-ha,' I said, forcing myself to sound as genuine as I possibly could.

'Turn you to ice in about five minutes flat, that would,' the steward said, still smiling broadly.

I felt as if her *words* had turned me to ice inside. 'Yes, I'm sure it would, ha ha,' I said woodenly.

I had to get away from here.

I walked off down the corridor as calmly and casually as I could.

Ding dong ding! An announcement came over the loudspeakers. 'Ladies and gentlemen, we regret to inform you that we shall not be leaving the port today, after all. The captain has checked the weather situation and unfortunately, it has taken another turn for the worse, with severe storms raging beyond the harbour. We will be staying in port for another day, while the storm passes. We do apologise, but this decision is for your own safety. We will provide extra entertainment and free excursions while we are docked. Once again, we are sorry for any inconvenience.'

I heard a few groans from disappointed families around me in the lounge. I didn't know whether to cheer or cry. Shona and the narwhal would be nearby, but, on the downside, we had to wait at least another day before getting away from Njord's mountain – and I had no idea how much trouble we would all be in once he unleashed the full extent of his anger.

Chapter Fourteen

*A*aron and I sat huddled around a table in the quietest corner of the lower deck's lounge. There were only a few others in there. Most of the guests had taken advantage of the offer of a free trip to a local fish farm.

A young couple were sitting in a window seat, arms wrapped round each other, looking out at the view; a family of four were playing a game of cards that looked complicated and loud. No one was paying us any attention.

'So what's the next step?' Aaron asked after

I'd filled him in on everything that had happened.

'Get the narwhal back to Neptune, I reckon. But don't ask me how.'

'We need to call him.'

'But we don't have either of our phones!'

Aaron rubbed his chin while he thought. 'Maybe we could use Mr Beeston's.'

'And risk telling Neptune that not only have we lost both of our phones, but I gave mine *away*! I'm not sure that's clever.'

'Well, let's at least tell Mr Beeston,' he said. 'If the narwhal was Neptune's most loyal pet, Mr Beeston will almost certainly know something about it. He might have some idea of how we can return it to Neptune.'

'Him, not it,' I said automatically – surprising myself with a feeling of affection as I thought about the narwhal.

'Him, then,' Aaron corrected himself. He thought for a moment. 'And what about the rest of it? The things that Njord told you, and what the guard said, too? If that's all true, we're no nearer to figuring out what's going on here than we were before.'

'I know. I mean, if Njord's telling the truth, and it was Neptune who turned him to ice, the *last* thing Neptune's going to want is for Njord to be brought back to life!'

'And we still don't know why Neptune has no memory of any of it,' Aaron said.

We fell silent. Neither of us had any answers to the hundreds of questions floating around.

'There you are!' Millie's voice boomed across the lounge. She marched towards us, Mr Beeston following behind her. 'We've been looking for you all day.'

'Well, not exactly all day,' Mr Beeston corrected her. 'Remember, I did tell you Emily and Aaron had been invited to play with a friend's family today.'

Millie smiled. 'Yes, of course, how silly of me to forget,' she said, pointedly folding her arms. 'Now, just remind me, what was the friend's name again?'

I froze for a second. Then quickly blurted, 'Sharon!'

At the exact same moment, Aaron said, 'Andrew!'

And just to top it off, Mr Beeston announced, 'Lorraine.'

Millie tightened her folded arms and frowned as she looked round at the three of us. 'Just as I thought,' she said. 'You're *all* lying. So, which one of you would like to begin the explanations?'

I looked at Mr Beeston, and then at Aaron. They both looked back at me, their faces saying the same thing that I was thinking: *how the heck do we get out of this?*

And then I decided how we'd get out of it. We'd tell the truth. It wasn't as if we had a lot to lose.

'Millie, I think you should sit down,' I said, pulling out a couple of chairs for her and Mr Beeston. 'I'm going to tell you everything.'

'You're serious?' Millie stared at me.

'Deadly serious,' I said.

She looked at the others. 'And you both knew about it?'

Aaron and Mr Beeston both nodded sheepishly.

She sucked on her teeth. 'I don't know what to say. I feel such a fool for being taken in like this. I bet you've had a right laugh behind my back, haven't you?'

'Millie, do we look like we're laughing?' I asked. 'We were given a task by Neptune, and we were told not to tell a single soul. Even Mr Beeston didn't know half of what we've just told you.'

'It's true,' Mr Beeston said. 'I was told I was to chaperone them; it's only now that I have been told the full extent of their mission.'

Millie stared at me for ages. Eventually, her face softened. 'All right,' she said. 'I understand. You poor things, carrying such a huge responsibility on your young shoulders.' Then she pushed her chair back and stood up.

'Where are you going?' I asked.

'I'm going to call Archie,' she said. 'He'll know what we should do.'

Aaron and I exchanged a quick look. Should we say something? Aaron gave me a quick nod.

'I don't think you should call Archie,' I said.

'Why ever not?'

'We don't think he can be trusted,' Aaron said.

I held my breath while Millie stared, open-mouthed, at Aaron.

'What in the name of the goddess makes you thin—'

'He was sneaking around on your boat,' I said.

'And remember how he reacted when he heard about our trip?' Aaron added.

Millie glared at us both. 'Is that it?' she said. 'Two tiny misunderstandings and you want to write him off?'

She had a point. It didn't really sound like much to go on.

So why was I so sure we were right?

Aaron was chewing his lip. 'There's something else,' he said. A line of blotchy red had spread up both of his cheeks. 'I don't know what you'll think when I tell you. You might turn against me as much as Emily did when I told her. But I've been thinking about it the whole time we've been here, and there's something about it that's not right.'

He glanced at me, raising his eyebrows as if to ask my permission. I nodded.

'He told me to kiss Emily,' Aaron said, in a quiet voice and looking down at the table.

'What has that got to do with—'

'It was when we kissed that we got our powers back,' I added, only now realising the full extent of what had happened. Maybe it hadn't just been about a bet.

'I don't know why he wanted it to happen,' Aaron went on. 'But he was really insistent that I should do it. As Neptune's closest advisor, I can't help thinking he must surely have known that this would give us some power over Neptune. I can't figure out why he would have wanted that – but something about it doesn't feel right.'

'Millie,' I said softly. 'I really don't think we can trust him.'

Millie was quiet for a long time. Finally, she nodded slowly, as if making a deal with herself. 'I'm sorry, but I think you're mistaken,' she said. 'I know Archie. He is the most decent, loving, kind, generous soul I know. I mean, look what he did for *me* – he managed to get me a place on this cruise holiday!'

'But maybe even that is part of it,' I said. 'He gave you a shell phone so you could keep in touch with him. Maybe the reason you're here is to spy on us!'

'Nonsense!' Millie snapped. 'No, I've had enough of this. You're wrong. I'm sure of it, and I won't listen to any more of your silliness. Archie is totally trustworthy, and I am off to call him now.'

With that, she flung her scarf over her shoulder and flounced out of the lounge. No one spoke for a few minutes.

Finally, Mr Beeston tried a smile. 'Well, that could have gone a lot worse,' he said feebly.

'Could it?' I asked. 'Really?'

In reply, he turned away and stared blankly out of the window. Aaron and I stared with him. Right then, it felt about the most useful thing we could do.

The next morning, it wasn't only the scenery that was frosty.

'Could you pass the salt, if you don't mind ever so much?' Millie asked with the coolness of an ice queen.

'Millie, please don't be like—'

'And the pepper, please.' She sliced into her bacon with such ferocity I wondered if she was imagining it to be one of us.

Mr Beeston put down his knife and fork. 'I suggest we all put yesterday behind us and try to be civil,' he said.

'Sounds good to me,' I agreed.

'Me, too,' Aaron added.

We waited for Millie to finish chewing. Finally, she wiped her mouth with her serviette, pursed her lips – and then, eventually, threw her hands in the air. 'Oh, all right then,' she said, with exasperation. 'You know I've never been one to cause a drama.'

Mr Beeston smiled. 'Right, good. That's that sorted.'

We ate in silence for a few minutes. I tried to think of something to say, but, to be honest, what with everything that was swimming around in my brain, I didn't have it in me to think up small talk.

'Anyone have any good dreams last night?' Aaron asked brightly.

I smiled gratefully at him.

Millie took a sip of her tea. 'Well, it's funny you should ask,' she said. 'Even by my own standards, my dreams have been rather interesting since we came on holiday. I mean, on . . . whatever this is.'

Ignoring her dig about the trip, I tried to show interest, for the sake of keeping her happy. 'Tell us,' I said, bracing myself for a lengthy, in-depth report of some crazy dream.

She shrugged. 'Nothing much to tell,' she said sniffily.

'Please, Millie. Tell us about your dream,' Mr Beeston said gently.

She let out a loud, dramatic sigh. 'Oh, very well then. If you insist.' Her eyes went all glassy and dreamy. 'It was a place, more than anything. Not a lot happened – but I had such a strong sense of the place.'

'What kind of place?' Aaron asked.

Millie looked out of the window. 'Icy cold, with snow-capped mountains, and in the middle of the mountains was a lake.'

I felt a sheet of ice go through me. A lake in the middle of mountains? Was Millie describing the place we'd been to? The lake of lost memories?

'You could see the reflections of all the mountains in the lake,' she went on. 'It was very beautiful.'

'Sounds like a lovely dream,' Mr Beeston said.

'It was. And the strange thing is, I've seen it before,' Millie said. 'It's a recurring dream that I've had about three or four times recently. But there was another thing this time – one of the mountains, the tallest of them all, which towered over the others . . . Her voice trailed away.

'What about it?' Aaron asked.

'It . . .' Millie's eyes had gone all misty and glassy. 'It was crying,' she said.

Aaron burst out laughing. I think it might have been nerves, but either way, it didn't help matters. 'A crying mountain?' he said. 'Oh, that's great!'

He carried on laughing for a few more moments, till he saw Millie's face. I knew it was probably nervous laughter – and it did sound a bit hysterical – but either way, Millie wasn't amused.

'I'm so glad you have decided to make fun of

197

me,' she said. 'That makes me feel *much* better about everything.'

'Millie, he's not making fun of you,' I said. 'He thought it was *meant* to be funny, didn't you, Aaron?'

Aaron gulped down some orange juice and nodded. 'I'm sorry,' he said.

'Any more dreams?' Mr Beeston asked brightly, trying hard to stop an all-out war.

'Well, yes, as it happens, I had another,' Millie said. 'I wonder if you'll find this one equally funny.'

'Go on,' Mr Beeston said.

'I saw a threat from the sky,' she told us. She turned to me, and for the first time since she'd flounced off yesterday, she looked at me with the love and care I was used to getting from Millie. 'It was coming for you,' she said.

I was glad I was sitting down, as my legs started shaking. The truth of it was, most of what Millie said turned out to be silly nonsense, but every now and then, she hit the nail on the head – as she had just done with her dream about the lake. I only hoped that she wasn't right about *this* one.

'Well, anyway. As I say, I'm sure it's just silly dreams,' Millie said quickly. Then she wiped her mouth and got up. 'I'm off to the buffet. Who's for seconds?'

'No thanks,' I said, getting up from the table. 'I need some air.' I pushed my chair in and excused myself.

'I'll come with you,' Aaron said.

We went up to the roof deck.

'What did you make of that, then?' Aaron asked as we leaned on the railings looking out at the sea still crashing in massive white explosions against the pier at the far end of the harbour.

'The description of the mountains and lake was a bit close to the truth,' I said.

'I know. Coincidence?'

I shrugged. 'I've no idea, but I think we really need to contact Neptune from Mr Beeston's shell phone – even if it means admitting what we've done with ours. There's too much at stake.'

'I agree,' Aaron said. 'Let's call him now.' He turned to go.

'In a minute,' I said. I wanted another moment alone with Aaron before facing Neptune's wrath.

We watched the spray of the swell and listened to the rumble from the sea further out. I had my hands in my coat pockets, keeping them out of the cold. My fingers closed around my last remaining crystal. I pulled it out of my pocket and looked at it.

'What am I going to do with this?' I asked. 'Do you think I should get rid of it, make sure it can't come to any harm?'

'I don't know, maybe we—'

He didn't get to finish his sentence. Out of nowhere, an enormous bird came swooping towards us. It looked familiar. The eagle again!

'What the—'Aaron jumped backwards, his hands over his head as the eagle brushed against his hair with the ends of its long wings.

It was heading straight for me. *A threat from the sky.*

Stumbling backwards, I tripped over a chair and lost my balance. As I landed awkwardly on my side, the crystal fell from my hand and rolled away from me.

Swooping so fast it was over in seconds, the eagle brushed down to the deck, picked up the crystal in its talons and flew off.

A moment later, Aaron was by my side. 'Are you OK?' he asked, reaching down to help me up.

I brushed myself down as I got to my feet. 'I'm fine,' I gasped, 'but the crystal has gone.'

Aaron scanned the deck.

'It's not there,' I said. 'The eagle took it.'

'Are you sure?'

'Positive. I saw it pick it up in its talons and fly off. Look!' I pointed into the distance where I could still see the eagle circling around the tops of the mountains. It flew round and round, drawing great, sweeping circles in the sky.

My stomach turned in a circle of its own as I realised where the eagle was heading. 'Aaron! I've seen that eagle before – when we were at the lake, and then when Shona and I left the mountain. It was there both times, circling.'

'You're sure it's the same one?'

'I can't be positive, but what if it is? What if it belongs to Njord?'

Aaron's face turned white. 'And it's heading straight back to him.'

'With the crystal.'

The eagle disappeared out of sight. It wouldn't take long for it to get back to the mountain. And as soon as it did, surely this would all be over. Njord would thaw, and then what? Would he come after us? What did he want, anyway? We had no idea – all we knew was that the idea of him returning to power was something so terrifying that it even scared Neptune. Beyond that, I didn't really want to think about it.

Which was just as well, because I didn't get the chance.

The water all around the ship suddenly began to bubble and seethe, even within the supposed safety of the harbour. The ship rocked and swayed, heaving up and down on sea that moments earlier had been relatively calm, but was now leaping about like water coming to the boil in a pan.

Surely this was too fast. Had the eagle already got back inside the mountain? Had Njord already thawed out?

The ship suddenly lurched to the side, and I fell against Aaron.

'What's going on?'

Aaron put an arm round me to steady me. I didn't complain. If Njord had become free and returned to power, our time might be limited, and I wasn't going to waste any of it pushing Aaron away when really that was the last thing I wanted to do.

Just as I was thinking this, the sea completely erupted. The ship lurched to the other side.

And then, from the eruption, came something familiar, something I hadn't expected at all, rising out of the ocean like a bright summer sunrise coming over the horizon.

Neptune.

Chapter Fifteen

A aron and I stared as the top of the trident and then the top of Neptune's head emerged from the sea.

Neptune shook water from his hair and looked directly up at us on the roof deck. Luckily, we were the only people around; everyone else was still in the dining room.

Neptune raised his hand and pointed to us, then to himself. 'Ten minutes,' he mouthed. And then he was gone.

I looked at Aaron. 'Did I just imagine that?'

Aaron shook his head. 'If you did, I imagined exactly the same thing.'

I really didn't relish the thought of having to face Neptune now, after we had so spectacularly failed at pretty much everything he'd asked us to do. But Neptune was generally used to getting his way about what he wanted. If he was telling us to be there in ten minutes, that was an order, not a polite request.

On the way down, we bumped into Mr Beeston and Millie leaving the dining room.

'Where are you two heading in such a hurry?' Mr Beeston asked as they approached us.

'Neptune is here,' I said. I didn't feel like keeping secrets any more. 'We're going to meet him.'

'Neptune? Here? Seriously?' Millie glanced all around and then bustled over to the window and looked out. 'Is he alone? Is Archie with him? I tried to call him last night but couldn't get through. Perhaps he was already on his way.'

'I've no idea,' I told her.

'All we know is that we have to go and meet him,' Aaron said.

Mr Beeston tightened his jacket and flattened down his hair. 'I'm coming with you.'

'What about me?' Millie asked. 'What can I do?'

'Cover for us,' Aaron said. 'Make sure no one sees us disappearing into the sea, and think of a really good story in case anyone notices we've gone.'

Millie pursed her lips. 'Well, off you go,' she said

briskly. 'You don't want to keep Neptune waiting.'

I gave Millie a hug. 'Thank you.'

She patted my back. 'Oh, go on with you,' she said gently. Then she managed a brief smile. 'Good luck.'

'We'd better get going,' said Mr Beeston. 'I don't need to tell any of you that Neptune is not known for his patience.'

He pulled a familiar-looking bottle of orange liquid out of his trouser pocket. I was about to ask what it was when I realised − it was the potion that Aaron and I used in the water. Mr Beeston was a semi-mer like us, so he'd need it too. I didn't say anything; I had the feeling it would only make him feel inferior if I did, as 'real' merpeople didn't need it. And right now, I didn't want to do anything to make Mr Beeston feel anything other than one hundred per cent on our side.

The three of us hurried off the boat and round to the bay where we could sneak into the water without being seen.

Neptune wasn't difficult to find. All around him, the sea burned in bright colours with flecks of gold amongst them − his chariot glowing in the centre of it all.

'Leave this to me.' Mr Beeston swam forward and bowed low in front of the chariot. 'Your Majesty,' he began. 'I know that we have so far failed to—'

Neptune waved his trident impatiently before Mr Beeston got any further. 'Save your explanations,' he boomed. 'I am not here to punish or to judge.'

That was a relief, but if he wasn't here to do either of those things, then what was he here for? Before I had a chance to ask him, someone emerged from behind Neptune: Archie!

'What's he doing here?' I spluttered.

'He insisted on joining me,' Neptune said. 'As I would expect, given that he's my closest aide.'

Someone else emerged from the shadows: Shona!

'What's *she* doing here?' Neptune boomed.

'I . . . she . . .' I began. And then stopped. I couldn't think of a single way to explain Shona's presence.

Shona swam straight up to Neptune and looked him in the eye. 'I knew Emily was in trouble,' she said firmly. 'She is my best friend, so I came.'

'But how . . .' Neptune's voice trailed off. Then he shook his head. 'It doesn't matter,' he said. 'Not any more. All that matters is the truth. That is why I'm here. I can no longer hide from my own story.'

'What about your dreams?' I asked. 'I thought they warned you it was too dangerous for you to come.'

'I have continued to dream since you left,' Neptune replied. 'And my most recent dreams told me that if I didn't come, the danger would be even greater.' He looked around at us all. 'So I am here – and yet, I am no closer to my history.'

'What do you mean?' I asked.

'I mean that it is still a black hole to me. I had thought perhaps it would come back once I was here, but whenever I try to recall my own story, I'm left with nothing but a void.'

At this point, Archie swam forward. 'Your Majesty, if I may say something . . .' he began. I glanced at Aaron, who rolled his eyes.

'Of course you may,' Neptune replied. 'You are my most trusted advisor. I will listen to anything you have to say.'

'We are here now,' Archie began. 'In the place where you believe you lost your memories. Surely, if there were ever a time for them to return, it would be now. If they haven't returned, perhaps it is because . . .' He paused.

'Because what?' Neptune asked impatiently.

'Forgive me, Your Majesty,' Archie went on. 'I hesitate to say this. I do not want to contradict you. But perhaps it is because the dreams were simply dreams – not memories at all.'

We fell silent as we waited for Neptune to respond. There was so much I wanted to say, but I didn't know where to start. Archie was totally wrong, but he had no way of knowing that – or did he?

It turned out I didn't have long to think about it. A smooth swishing noise came from behind Shona. Something was approaching.

The narwhal!

I'm back.

It swam straight over to the chariot and dipped its head. A second later, Archie darted in between the narwhal and Neptune. He pulled a long sword from the side of his tail.

His voice shook as he turned to Neptune and asked, 'Shall I kill it?'

'NO!' I swam forwards – leaping in front of Archie and his sword. I turned to the narwhal. 'Are you OK?'

Don't worry about me.

Archie stared at me. His face had drained of colour. He looked scared! Was he scared of the narwhal?

'He won't hurt you,' I said, swimming to the narwhal's side. 'He's our friend. He's on our side.' I looked up at Neptune. 'Please don't let Archie hurt him,' I added.

Neptune had turned as white as his beard. 'The . . . the . . . my . . .'

With a lightning swift flick of his head, the narwhal knocked Archie's sword from his hand and swam to Neptune.

'My narwhal,' Neptune said. Then he began to laugh. 'I remember you, my friend.' Closing his hands over the top of the narwhal's head, Neptune kissed the top of his tusk. 'Bring them back!' he ordered. 'Bring my memories back!'

The narwhal tipped his head forward, lowering his tusk. Neptune bowed his head to allow the narwhal's tusk to touch his forehead. As he did so, the energy around them began to crackle. Sparks flew all around; lights glinted on the water beside them, dancing and leaping on the crests of the waves and wrapping them both in a spiral of colour and light.

Finally, the lights swirled upwards, whooshed into a point above Neptune's head and in a final *puff!* disappeared altogether.

One hand resting gently on the narwhal's head, Neptune looked around at us all. His face had changed. He looked as if a hundred years of stress had been taken away from him.

'I remember,' he said.

'You remember what?' Archie asked nervously.

Neptune smiled. And then, in a quiet, calm voice, he said, 'Everything.'

'Many, many hundreds of years ago, the oceans were ruled very differently,' Neptune began. 'Those early days of my childhood were the days when I learned everything. My parents ruled the seas back then. *Our* parents.'

He paused and looked to the sky, as if he might find a vision of his early family life there. 'But those days came to an abrupt end when our mother and father died,' he went on. 'My brother Njord and I wept together over our aged parents as they lay, side by side, dying. But my father did not approve of his sons crying, and he would not allow our tears to fall into the oceans. In his dying moments, he created an island like no other. An island formed of mountains: giant, jagged peaks that reached higher into the sky than anything anyone had seen before.'

We listened, enthralled, as Neptune went on.

'He sent our tears away to the tops of these mountains, and then he turned them to ice. He told us he did not want us to show such weakness ever again, and he made us promise we would honour this final, dying wish.'

'Which of course, you did,' said Mr Beeston. 'We have all only ever known Neptune as the strong ruler he is today.'

Neptune frowned and carried on. 'Of course we made this promise,' he said tersely. 'In exchange, father made one concession to our tears. The ones that lay within the thickest layers of ice at the top of the highest mountain would retain a magic that would keep both of us safe from danger. No one could touch this water except for us – and it would help us, should harm ever come to either Njord or me.'

'I get it,' I said. 'The water that melted when the midnight sun shone on it — that was your magic water. That's why we could catch it — because we had your power.'

'And why it burned anyone else who tried to touch it,' Aaron added.

Neptune gave us a quick nod before carrying on. 'After my parents had passed away, the years of uneasy rule began. My brother and I never saw things in the same way. Neither of us was ever happy with his share, and both fought for more. But while, on my part, the fighting was limited to raging arguments, Njord determined that he was going to take things a step further.'

'What did he do?' Aaron asked.

'It wasn't what he *did*, it was what he *tried* to do — and, luckily, I had enough spies in his camp to stop him before he managed to put his plan into action.'

'What was the plan?' I asked.

'He wanted to create a tsunami. The biggest wave the world had ever seen — bigger than all of the mountains in the range our parents had created.' Neptune shook his head, as if he couldn't quite believe what he was saying. 'The wave was to be set in motion, perfectly positioned and perfectly timed so that, eventually, it would flood all of the lands.'

'All of the lands? What do you mean, "all of the lands"?' I asked.

Neptune met my eyes. 'I mean exactly what you think I mean. His greed was unimaginable. His reasoning was beyond comprehension. He thought that if we were not satisfied with the amount of sea each of us had to rule, the only solution was to create more. He wanted to wipe out the land completely – turn everything to sea.'

I let out a breath. Njord had wanted to virtually destroy the planet! Turn it all into one big ocean and leave no trace of land at all! How could anyone think like that?

'My spies told me of his plan the night before it was due to take effect. I tried to reason with Njord. I fought, argued, I even begged him. He merely laughed in my face and told me to go away. It was then that I realised I had lost my brother. This was not someone I could call family; this was not someone I could do *anything* with. He had to be stopped – that was all that mattered.'

'So you turned him to ice,' Aaron said.

'I'm not proud of what I did, but I had so little time to act. When I turned my brother and his kingdom to ice, a part of *me* turned to ice with him. I told no one what I had done, and the pain of it was unbearable; I had lost my parents, and now I had lost my brother. More than that, I had lost my faith. I could never again trust anyone or anything.

I could never be happy, knowing what I had done. And how could I face my people and my oceans and have them accept me as their ruler, when I could not accept myself?'

I suddenly realised I knew who had taken Neptune's memories.

'You wiped your own memory,' I said.

Neptune lowered his head. 'What else could I do? Njord could not be allowed to put his plan into action – but I could not rule with the knowledge of what I had done.'

'How did you do it?' Aaron asked.

Neptune indicated for the narwhal to come nearer. He swam in closer to Neptune's side.

'The narwhal,' he said simply.

'But how?' I asked.

'I asked him to pierce my mind with his tusk and take my memories away.'

Aaron let out a low whistle. 'He can do that?'

Neptune smiled. 'This narwhal is a most magical and special creature. He can do many things.'

'What did he do with your memories?' I asked.

'I told him to take them away to a place where they would never again be found. Then he was to gather my loyal servants – the spies in Njord's camp – and bring them back to me. That was my terrible mistake. In sending him to fetch my loyal followers, I had unthinkingly sent the narwhal deep inside the very mountain which was in the process of turning to ice. In carrying out my wishes, my precious narwhal became enfolded in the big freeze.'

We all fell silent, and for a moment, it felt as if everything might turn out all right after all. Neptune had remembered everything, and seemed kind of OK with it; his beloved pet had been returned; Archie was here by Neptune's side and clearly not out to cause any trouble – and there was no sign of Njord, so the eagle obviously hadn't taken the crystal to him after all. It must have just flown off with it, leaving Njord still frozen inside the mountain.

All in all, it seemed as though we'd done a pretty good job, and perhaps we could all go home. I was about to say so, when something stopped me.

A rumbling sound. It seemed to be coming from all around us, making the ocean froth like a milkshake in a blender. Even the sea floor was vibrating beneath us.

I grabbed Aaron's arm. 'What's happening?'

'I don't know.'

The swell was starting to throw all of us around, even Neptune and his chariot were being rocked from side to side.

'Hold my hand,' Aaron said. 'Perhaps we can fight it.'

I took Aaron's hand and gripped it tightly. Nothing changed. If anything, a bigger surge swept through the water. A black ray flapped by, its fins hitting me in the face. A jellyfish splattered against my tail. Rocks and stones and plants were being uprooted from the seabed itself.

Then the ocean turned into a giant whirlpool; a vortex, picking us all up, spinning us round and propelling us to the surface of the bubbling ocean.

Wiping our faces, pulling hair out of our eyes, gasping for breath, we looked around to see what was happening.

For a moment, the sea continued to attack us, huge balls of water rising up from below us into the air, only to come crashing down all around us. It was as if a furious giant was hurling rocks made of sea water across the ocean.

And then it stopped. Just like that. No movement, no fury, no nothing. Just a still, calm sea, surrounded by mountains on one side and a frozen glacier on the other, with a blue sparkling fjord just beyond. It was as though the mayhem had never happened.

I looked around at the others. Everyone looked bedraggled and confused, but they were all still here.

'Now what?' I asked.

The answer came from a long way away – from the fjord on the other side of the glacier.

'Now, we FIGHT!'

Njord! He had risen out of the sea and was calling to us.

Neptune raised his head and looked over at his brother. I had no idea of the thoughts going through his head, but if the expression on his face was anything to go by, brotherly make-up hugs were not likely to be first on the agenda.

'It is time to end our quarrel for good,' Njord boomed. 'And the only way to do it is with a fight to the death!'

Neptune continued to stare at his brother. 'If that is your choice, so be it,' he said eventually.

'I shall give you today to prepare,' Njord said. 'We meet back here at midnight, and fight for our future.'

'Very well,' said Neptune. 'The winner shall rule all of the oceans himself. And the loser . . .'

'The loser shall DIE!' Njord bellowed.

Everything fell silent. It was as if the sea stopped moving, the sky froze, the wind fell.

And then Neptune replied.

'Agreed!' he growled.

Njord let out a horrible, cackling laugh, before disappearing back to wherever he'd come from.

Neptune turned to us. 'All of you, leave me be,' he said. 'I have had a long journey. If I am to battle against my brother tonight, I need some rest.'

'Can we do anything at all?' Aaron asked.

Neptune shook his head. 'This is between my brother and me,' he said.

But something was bothering me: a horrible feeling creeping up inside. A feeling that this was all our fault. 'Wait!' I said.

Neptune turned to face me.

'I mean – wait, please, Your Majesty.'

'What is it?' Neptune asked.

'I just need to know something.'

'Very well. Ask.'

I hesitated. I didn't want him to confirm that Aaron and I had completely messed everything up, but I needed to know.

'If we had never come here, Njord would have stayed frozen, and you would never have known about it,' I said. 'Things would have carried on perfectly peacefully. Was this whole journey a waste of time? Or is it even worse than that? Have we *caused* all of this by coming here?'

Neptune looked softly at me. 'You couldn't be further from the truth,' he said. 'The midnight sun falling on the mountains each year was beginning to melt Njord. It was happening very slowly – but it *was* happening. Njord would have become free at some point.'

'When?' asked Aaron.

'Who knows?' Neptune replied. 'It could have been next year; it could have been fifty years from now. All I know is that it *would* have happened – and there would have been no one here to stop him. Because of you, we are *all* here – and we stand at least a chance of fighting his evil plans.' He smiled at Aaron and me. 'You have fought a brave battle,' he said kindly. 'Now we have to ensure we win the war.' With that, he beckoned Archie to join him in the chariot. 'Come Archie, let's go.'

As the dolphins began to pull the chariot away, Neptune turned back to us. 'Stay safe,' he said. 'I'll see you at midnight.'

Chapter Sixteen

*T*he rest of the day passed in a blur. At some point, we went back to the ship. Shona stayed with the narwhal and we went inside to bring Millie up to date with events. It didn't go too well. When Millie heard that Archie was around but hadn't been able to come to see her, she was devastated.

Well, she was in good company. There weren't many smiles going around *any* of us for the rest of the day. We had an early dinner and decided we should all get some rest before meeting up with Neptune later.

Millie and I went back to our cabin and set an alarm for half past eleven in case we fell asleep. Millie was asleep in minutes and lay on her back, mouth open, snoring heavily as usual. I stared at the ceiling, my mind too busy and too full of questions to even allow my eyes to close.

I must have drifted off without realising it though, as a soft tapping sound woke me with a start some time later. I jumped out of bed and crept to the door. I looked down the corridor. No one was there. I must have imagined it.

I was about to get back into bed when I heard it again. This time I realised it was coming from the porthole. I leaned across to look out of the big round window. Someone was out there. I craned my neck to see who it was.

Archie! What did he want?

He jabbed a finger towards the back of the boat and mouthed something at me. He was telling me to meet him. 'Bring Aaron,' he mouthed, then held up his hand to indicate five minutes.

I silently let myself out of the cabin and went to find Aaron.

We leaned over the railings on the lowest deck and listened to what Archie had to say.

'I haven't got long,' he began. 'I don't want Neptune to know I'm here.'

'I bet you don't,' I said before I could stop myself.

He looked at me. 'What's that supposed to mean?'

I bit my lip.

'She means we don't trust you,' Aaron said. 'We've been talking about some of the things that you've done – and they don't add up.'

'What things?'

'That time I saw you at Millie's behaving oddly, and the way you reacted when you heard about us going on this trip,' I told him.

'And when you told me to kiss Emily,' Aaron said, blushing furiously. 'We don't know exactly what your game is, but we think you're up to something.'

For a moment, Archie didn't say anything. Then he held up both hands. 'OK, you've got me in a corner,' he said. 'I'm going to tell you the truth.'

Whatever I might have been expecting him to say, that hadn't been it. I thought he'd at least try to deny it. And if I'm honest, I'd hoped we'd been wrong. I wanted there to be a perfectly reasonable explanation for his odd behaviour, but it seemed we'd been right all along: Archie wasn't to be trusted, and he was about to confess all.

'I knew about Neptune's story before he did,' Archie began.

'How come?' I asked.

'There is a line of merfolk: a very secret, very select group. I come from this line.'

'Who are they? What makes them so special?' Aaron asked.

'We are the ones who know the full truth. We are the ones who keep the peace.'

'You're the ultimate peacekeeper?' I asked. 'What if we find that hard to believe?'

Archie raised his shoulders in a slow shrug. 'Then I wouldn't blame you. All I ask is that you hear me out.'

Aaron and I exchanged a look. Aaron nodded. 'Go on, then,' I said.

'I first saw you when you stood up to Neptune in his own court. You impressed us all. My superiors told me we had to watch you.'

'Watch me?' I burst out. 'As in, spy on me, like Mr Beeston did for almost all my life?'

'Not spy on you, no,' Archie said quickly. 'We just wanted to keep someone near you, see how things progressed. We had the feeling you might be special. It turned out we were right.'

'You mean, when you came into our lives, it wasn't a coincidence?'

'No, not exactly.'

'And when you started going out with Millie, that was . . .'

Archie at least had the decency to look

embarrassed. 'I care very much about Millie,' he said. 'But—'

'But the whole thing was a big, fat pack of lies!' The voice came from behind me. I spun round.

'Millie!' Archie probably should have tried a bit harder to hide the horror on his face. As it was the first time he'd seen his so-called girlfriend in days, his usual look of soppy adoration would probably have gone down better.

'I heard Emily talking to someone in our cabin,' Millie said, her voice lifeless and dull. 'It crossed my mind that it might be you, but, no, surely it couldn't be. You would never have come all this way and made no attempt to see me – your beloved!'

'Millie, I—'

'So I pretended to be asleep,' Millie went on, ignoring him. 'I followed her, and this is what I found – that my whole relationship has been nothing but make-believe.'

I couldn't help glancing at Aaron. I knew how she felt! He turned away and wouldn't meet my eyes.

'Millie, I might have met you in somewhat unusual circumstances, but that doesn't make our relationship any less real,' Archie said.

'Our *relationship* no longer exists!' Millie spat. She turned to me. 'Emily, I'm sorry. I should have believed you.'

'Millie, please!' Archie begged.

Millie swung round to face him again. 'That's a thought,' she said. 'What exactly *were* you doing in my home that day? The truth, this time.'

'All right, then,' Archie said. 'I'll tell you. I was looking at your diaries.'

Millie gasped. 'You were *what*?'

'You know how sometimes we would tell each other about our dreams?'

Millie folded her arms and pursed her lips together in reply.

'Sometimes you said things that were familiar to me,' Archie went on. 'You described scenes I had heard of, scenes my family had told me about in stories passed from generation to generation. We treasured those stories more than our lives. You described places that to us were sacred. Places you had never even been to.'

'This still doesn't explain why you were sneaking about in my home,' Millie said firmly.

'You told me you always wrote your dreams down in a book. I needed that book. We knew that time was running out. Neptune was troubled, and I suspected what was happening.'

'I suppose you'd been spying on him, too,' Millie said sharply.

Archie ignored her and carried on. 'I need you to understand where I'm coming from. I am not the enemy. I'm possibly the only one who can save

Neptune from certain death. And you have to help me.'

'Are you saying you think Neptune is going to lose the fight with his brother?' Aaron asked.

Archie shook his head. 'I'm saying I *know* Neptune will lose the fight. If we don't stop this from happening, Neptune will die at midnight tonight.'

'What makes you so sure?' I demanded.

'I know Njord's methods. Before he was turned to ice, my folk followed his movements for many generations. He doesn't play by the rules, he makes up his own as he goes along – and believe me, they are dirty. Neptune doesn't stand a chance.'

Millie edged closer to the railing and knelt down. 'So . . . so you mean, all this time, all the secrets . . . it's all been to support Neptune?'

Archie edged closer and looked up into her eyes. 'Totally. I just couldn't tell you any of this before, as our operation is the most secret one there is. Even Neptune doesn't know about it.'

'Why not?' I asked. I wasn't completely ready to let go of my suspicions yet.

'Can you imagine how he'd feel if he knew there was an elite group whose sole aim was to keep him from harm? How would his ego cope with that?' Archie replied. 'Besides, Neptune deliberately took away his own memories. How could I reveal the truth without reminding him of everything he had chosen to forget? It would have destroyed him.'

'But now you're saying *Njord* will destroy him?' I said.

'Not if we can help it.' Archie turned back to Millie. 'Darling, I'm sorry about the way this has all come out. I know that the manner of our getting together might have had more to do with my work than anything else – but everyone knows that you became more than work to me. You are my sunrise, my full moon, my—'

'I forgive you!' Millie exclaimed, blowing a kiss down to him. 'I understand. Oh, darling, you are still my hero.'

Archie beamed, and blew a kiss back to Millie.

I had to confess, his story did sound plausible. There was just one thing still troubling me. 'Why did you need to keep an eye on me in the first place?' I asked.

'From your first speech in Neptune's court, we knew that you were someone with the potential to help,' Archie said. 'Someone we might need if Neptune ever came to be in real danger. And you turned out to be more valuable than we had ever dreamed.'

'You mean because Aaron and I found the rings and got Neptune's power?'

'Exactly. After that, we knew that if Neptune's power was ever taken away, we still had you to save him from whatever threat he was facing.'

'Which was why you were so keen to help us get our power back, once we'd lost it,' Aaron put in.

Archie met his eyes, and then mine. 'Exactly,' he said. 'I didn't know if it would work, but I knew it was worth a try.'

My head was spinning. I didn't know what to think any more.

'My whole life has been leading up to this moment,' Archie said. 'You have to help Neptune, your king. And you *have* to believe me.'

Aaron looked at me, and I nodded. Archie was telling the truth, I could see that now. He was desperate to keep Neptune out of trouble. I couldn't doubt him any more. And he was right about something else – we had to help.

'We believe you,' Aaron said.

'Oh, my Archie, my brave, clever darling,' Millie squealed. 'I'm so proud of you!'

Archie smiled broadly at all of us, the relief plain on his face. 'Thank goodness,' he said. 'OK, listen. There's no time to waste. Millie, wait for me. I will come back for you. Emily and Aaron, come and join me down here and let me tell you my plan.'

'I've been thinking hard about this, and there's only one way to do it,' Archie said, once Aaron and I had got off the ship and joined him in the water. 'We have to get the narwhal to take away both Neptune and Njord's memories. If neither of them can remember ever falling out, they can rule the seas between them – and no one needs to die.'

'That sounds like a good plan. How do we do it?' asked Aaron.

Archie turned to me. 'You can hear the narwhal's thoughts, can't you?'

'How did you know?'

'I saw you. When it came back. You spoke to it, didn't you?'

I nodded. 'I spoke to *him*.'

'As I thought. It will be up to you, then.'

'What do you want her to do? I'm not letting you put her in any danger,' Aaron warned – which was kind of sweet, but also kind of not really his decision.

'Just tell me what I have to do,' I said.

'Take the narwhal to Neptune while he's sleeping. Tell him to pierce the king's thoughts as he did before, tell him to take away all the memories of his argument with his brother. After that, we must take away our memories of all these events as well.'

'What about Millie?' I asked.

'Hers too. We shall bring the narwhal to meet her at the shoreline and do it there.'

'And Njord?' I asked. 'Do I have to take the narwhal to him, too?' I couldn't help a shiver running through me as I thought about that. How was I going to face him? Did Archie expect me to creep up on him and double-cross him while he slept? I didn't think I could do it.

'Just tell the narwhal to listen to my instructions on that. I will take him to Njord. It's far too dangerous for you to attempt it.'

I breathed a sigh of relief. 'Thank you.'

'OK, let's get on with it,' Aaron said. The sooner we get started, the sooner we—'

'There's one more thing.' Archie looked uncomfortable.

'What?' I asked.

'I haven't told you what you have to do next.' He looked awkward now, turning away and refusing to meet my eyes.

I was worried now. 'What?'

'You have to take the narwhal away,' he said.

Why had he found that so difficult to say? 'Fine, just let me know where I need to take him and I'll do that.'

Archie finally met my eyes. 'Emily, you have to lead him to his death.'

No one spoke for a moment. I think we all assumed we'd heard wrong. 'Say that again?' I murmured at last.

'You heard right,' Archie said. 'We have to take away all of our memories and make sure that they *never* come back. And that's the only way.'

'I won't do it.'

'Emily, you have to, otherwise this battle between the brothers will go on for ever. And I promise you it won't end well for Neptune.'

I was about to argue, but then I heard a voice.

Do it.

I looked around. A familiar shape was coming closer: the narwhal.

Do what he says. He is right – it is the only way.

'No! I can't do it; you've done nothing wrong. It's not fair!'

Please, do not worry about me. I am prepared to lay down my life for Neptune. It would be an honour. Please. We have no choice.

I turned to Archie and, eventually, I nodded. Let him think I would do it, but I knew in my heart that I wouldn't let the narwhal die – I *couldn't*. I had no idea how I would stop it – but I'd think of something. I had to.

Chapter Seventeen

I watched as the narwhal took away Neptune's memories. Holding his tusk against Neptune's forehead, sparks and colours silently flowed around the pair of them while Neptune slept – unaware of any of it.

When it was over, I followed the narwhal along the dark tunnels that led to the place where Archie had told us to meet him.

'Is it done?' Archie asked.

I nodded.

'Everyone?'

'Everyone,' I confirmed. 'There's just you, me and Njord to go.'

'Well done. I'll take the narwhal to Njord now. I will get him to remove Njord's memories, and then my own. Meet me back here in twenty minutes. Bear in mind, when I see you again, I won't remember why we're here. Put your faith in the narwhal. He'll lead you where you need to go.'

'I'll be waiting for you,' I said. 'Please, be quick.'

Archie nodded, and then he turned and swam away. I watched as he and the narwhal disappeared into the pitch darkness of the tunnel.

Twenty minutes later, they were back.

'Hey, Emily! How did you get here?' Archie said, all smiles.

'You told me to meet you,' I replied. 'I'm exactly where I was last time I saw you!'

Archie looked at me quizzically. 'Huh? Last time I saw you was in Brightport!'

Wow! This was really it, then. The narwhal had taken away Archie's memory. A shiver ran through me. It was all down to me, now; I was the only one who knew the truth of all this.

'Oh, yes, ha ha,' I said. 'Just kidding. I'm here on holiday. How about you?'

'Official duties. I'm here with Neptune. Don't even ask me why – I have no idea! I think he fancied a trip north.'

Just then, the narwhal swam out from behind Archie.

'Wow, a narwhal!' Archie breathed. 'You don't often see them. They're extremely rare, you know.'

'Really?' I said in my best *well-I-had-no-idea-about-that-at-all* voice.

The narwhal swam over and nuzzled against me.

'It likes you.'

'Mm.'

Archie nudged a thumb in the direction of Neptune's quarters. 'Anyway, nice to see you. I'd better go and check on the boss.'

With that, he was gone, and I was left in the dark tunnel with only the narwhal and the awful knowledge of my task for company – the task that I promised myself I would not do, no matter what happened.

The narwhal and I swam off together. The worst of it was that he seemed to know the way. He knew exactly where he had to go in order to face his own death. Well, *he* might be resigned to his fate, but I still wasn't. I would think of a way around it, I swore it.

We swam past weird see-through creatures with long feathery legs and filaments sparkling all around their bodies. We swam past rocks covered in pale yellow shrubs and big green plants that looked like giant cabbages. We swam past a shoal of fish so big it turned the sea black as it came towards us. On and on we swam, until the surroundings began to feel familiar.

We were in the tunnels Shona and I had used when we came out of Njord's mountain with the narwhal the first time – the ones that led to the deep pool that Njord and his guards didn't even know about.

The ones that *no one* knew about.

That was it! The perfect solution!

I kicked hard with my tail and caught up with the narwhal. 'Stop! I've got an idea. We don't have to do this!'

The narwhal turned and raised his head.

'Take me to the secret pool at the end of these tunnels,' I said. 'No one knows about it. I could leave you there.'

The narwhal didn't move. Did he understand what I was saying? He tilted his head to the side, as if he were trying to communicate with me – but still he didn't say anything. 'Take me to the pool,' I said again. 'Please.'

The narwhal didn't move for a moment. And then he bowed his head, turned and led the way.

Together, we swam in silence through secret tunnels, through dark crevasses and hairline cracks, to the biggest secret at the very heart of Njord's mountain.

I put my arms round the narwhal's head and kissed the top of his tusk. 'Will you be all right down here, all on your own?'

The narwhal nodded. I guessed he must have been too choked up to speak. I almost was, myself.

'Hide here for a bit: a few days, maybe a week, just to be sure,' I said. 'Once Neptune and Njord are friends again and this is all over, they'll leave here and you can come out again. You'll be free.'

I looked into his tiny black eyes, stroked his speckly grey head. He looked beautiful, and sad. His eyes seemed to be saying something, but still he wouldn't speak.

'Stay safe,' I said. He pressed his head against mine. I kissed his forehead. 'It's time. Take all my memories away.' I stumbled on my words as the tears clogged up my throat. 'Make sure you remove them all, so there's no chance that I can ever betray you.'

My tears were flowing freely now. And then I noticed – I wasn't the only one crying.

I reached out to wipe a tear from the narwhal's eye. He turned away from me, probably embarrassed that I'd seen him cry. As he turned, I felt something happening in my hand. I looked down.

The narwhal's tear had hardened and turned into a crystal! It sparkled and glowed in my palm. I quickly closed my fingers around it and shoved it into my coat pocket. Once the narwhal had taken my memories away, I wouldn't know what it was –

but even if it would no longer remind me of him, at least I'd get to keep something beautiful from having known him.

I gave him one final hug. 'Bye,' I whispered. Then I curled my tail round, lowered my head, closed my eyes and waited for him to touch me with his tusk.

A moment later, I felt a tiny scratch and a dull pressure on my forehead.

'I'll never forget you,' I said – even though I knew I was wrong. As soon as the magic took effect and I was out of here, I *would* forget him. That was the whole point.

The midnight sun shone down on me as I swam back to the ship. I was so tired. Fancy choosing to come out in the middle of the night for a swim! I laughed to myself, flipped my tail and dived underwater.

Shaking my tail dry, I sat on the pebbly beach near the harbour, waiting for my legs to come back. Then I headed back to the ship and made my way to my cabin.

Millie was in bed already, asleep and snoring as usual. As I undressed for bed, something fell from my jacket. I bent down to pick it up. What was this? It looked like some sort of crystal. As I held it in my hand, it sparkled and shone, sprinkling light around the cabin. Where on earth had this come from?

I shoved it in my drawer. I was too tired to do anything about it now. All I wanted to do was get some sleep.

I'd think about the crystal in the morning.

'Emily, wake up!'

I prised an eye open. Millie was leaning over me, shaking me by the arm.

'Oh, good, you're awake,' she said, smiling brightly. 'Come on, let's go.'

'Go where?'

'Breakfast. First sitting. And then we're off out with Archie. He's sending a boat for us. Says he's got a treat for us before the ship moves on.'

'Swishy!' I jumped out of bed, got dressed and followed Millie down to breakfast.

'So, kids. What do you fancy doing today?' Mr Beeston asked as he spread a thick layer of marmalade on his toast. 'Captain says we'll be moving off this afternoon, now the storms finally seem to have passed.'

'Millie says Archie's got a treat for us,' I said.

'Sounds good to me.' Mr Beeston wiped his mouth. He had a bit of marmalade on his chin, but I didn't point it out. 'Everyone enjoying the holiday?'

'Totally!' Aaron said.

'Absolutely!' I added.

'Couldn't be better,' Millie said, as she sipped her tea.

I wolfed down my breakfast as quickly as I could. I couldn't wait to find out what kind of treat Archie had in store for us.

Half an hour later, we were in a small bay, round the headland and out of sight of the ship. Millie sat in a little boat, leaning over the side to kiss and cuddle with Archie. He grinned up at her. Honestly, those two – could they ever give it a rest?

Aaron and I were in the water with Mr Beeston. Shona had joined us too. She'd come on holiday here as well, so she could be near us.

It wasn't long before we saw something coming towards us. Something very familiar. Neptune! What was *he* doing here?

He was in his chariot – and there was someone else with him. Wait – was I seeing double? The other person was the image of Neptune!

They rode towards us, both grinning broadly and talking animatedly.

Neptune slipped from the chariot and held out a hand towards his mirror image. 'I would like to introduce you to someone very special,' he said. 'This is my twin brother.'

His *what*?

'My long lost, beloved brother, Njord.' He turned to his brother. 'We haven't seen each other in . . . how long is it now?'

'I can't remember,' the mirror image – Njord – replied.

Neptune burst out laughing. 'Neither can I! And what's more, I don't care, either! What I care about is that you're here now. And that deserves a celebration.'

Njord got out of the chariot and put an arm round Neptune. 'My dear brother,' he said, smiling. 'I couldn't agree more. Let's have a party!'

Neptune thrust his trident in the air. 'A party – that's *exactly* what we'll have! I order it! Midday, everyone back here. We will celebrate in style.'

And with that, the two brothers got back in the chariot, and rode off, talking, laughing and slapping each other on the back all the way.

'Wow, Archie certainly knows how to plan a treat,' Aaron said.

'Doesn't he just. I can't wait for the party,' I agreed.

'Nice thing to do before we carry on with the holiday,' Mr Beeston added.

'Come on,' Aaron said, flicking water at me with his tail as he turned and began to swim away. 'Race you back to the ship.'

We swam along together, laughing and splashing

each other. This holiday really *was* turning out to be the trip of a lifetime.

Once we got back to the ship, I went to my cabin to get ready for the party. I caught sight of myself in the mirror – my hair was in a terrible state! I opened my drawer, looking for my brush.

What was *that*?

The inside of my drawer was glowing. It looked like a light flowing through a kaleidoscope. White smoke, swirling and curling, filling the whole drawer with a flickering, dancing light. It seemed to be coming from something at the back of the drawer. I reached inside and felt around. My fingers closed round something hard: a crystal. I vaguely remembered putting it in my drawer last night, but I had no idea where I'd got it from.

As I held it in my palm, I got a really weird feeling. I couldn't put my finger on it – what was it? It felt like sadness, but there was more than that, too. A strong feeling of – of what? I know it sounds stupid, but it felt like family – like someone I loved was saying my name. I turned the crystal over and over in my hand.

The longer I held it, the more it pulled at me.

Follow me.

I spun round. Where had that voice come from?

I looked back at my outstretched palm. I knew I was probably going crazy for even thinking it, but the voice seemed to have come from the crystal! 'Was that you?' I whispered, feeling a tiny bit stupid and glad that there was no one around to hear me talking to my hand!

Follow me. It sounded like an echo.

I closed my cabin door behind me, and, clutching the crystal tightly inside my pocket, I went to find Aaron and Shona.

I found Aaron in the lounge, playing cards with Mr Beeston and Millie.

'Come with me,' I whispered in his ear.

Mr Beeston waved his hands. 'It's fine. You kids go and play,' he said with a smile.

'What is it?' Aaron asked as he followed me down the corridor and off the boat.

'Just come,' I said.

We sneaked back into the sea and swam round to the little bay where Shona was staying.

Once we were all together and definitely out of sight of the ship, I showed them the crystal. It glowed and sparkled in my hand, exploding with light like a firework. The lights seemed to form an arrow, pointing out towards the open sea.

'Wow!' Aaron said. 'It looks like it's drawing a path in the sea.'

'I know. Let's follow it and see where it takes us!' I suggested.

'Swishy!' Shona said, grinning. 'An adventure!'

We set off together, me in front, holding the crystal out in my hand and letting it draw its bright lines in the water. We followed as it glowed and shone, leading us through the blue, blue fjord, across the open sea and towards a beautiful range of snow-capped mountains.

This was going to be a fun day!

The crystal brought us closer to the mountains and took us down dark tunnels that twisted and snaked, deeper and deeper with every swish of our tails. It felt as if we were swimming right through the middle of a mountain!

'This is spooky,' Shona said.

'Yeah, but fun,' Aaron added.

We carried on swimming through the darkness, the only light coming from the crystal – leading us on. Finally, we came back out into the light.

'Wow! How beautiful is this?' Shona gasped.

Our tunnel had become a river, winding into a shimmering, sparkling lake surrounded by a circle of mountains. Everything was totally still. The sun's rays filtered down through the surface of the lake, spreading out like a fan under the water.

'What are *they*?' Shona asked, pointing ahead of us.

'They look like bubbles,' Aaron said.

Bubbles? Bubbles inside a lake? There was something familiar about this, but I couldn't think what. I couldn't have been here before or I would've remembered. Maybe I'd dreamed about it.

'Let's check them out,' Aaron suggested.

He and I approached one of the bubbles. Instinctively, Aaron reached out for my hand, and I took it. With my other hand, I reached out to touch the bubble. It felt weird.

'It's like jelly!' I said.

Aaron reached out and touched the bubble. As he did, it melted away and disappeared; in its place was an image. It was Aaron and Archie! They were talking. I felt as if I was watching them on an old movie screen. I leaned in closer to hear what they were saying.

'Go on, I dare you. You know you want to,' Archie was saying.

'Stop it,' Aaron replied. 'Leave me alone.'

Archie grinned and nudged Aaron in the ribs. 'I bet you a tenner you're too chicken.'

'I'm not chicken at all.'

'Then do it. Kiss her tonight! Ten pounds says you won't do it.'

Aaron's face was bright red as he met Archie's eyes. With anger or embarrassment? I couldn't tell. 'I was planning to kiss her, anyway,' he said. 'And it's not because of you or your bet. It's because I *want* to. You can keep your money. I don't want it. All I want is for Emily to be my girlfriend.'

The image faded.

I looked at Aaron. I suddenly remembered a huge argument. How could I have forgotten?

He was looking back at me with shock in his eyes. 'Emily, I–I'd completely forgotten about this,' he said. 'How *could* I have forgotten? We fought about it, didn't we? But. Em, this isn't why I kissed you. I didn't do it for a bet, I promise. I—'

'Shh,' I said. 'It's OK, I believe you. I know you would never have done something like that for a bet. And anyway, the argument was partly my fault too.'

'How d'you figure that out?'

'I should never have doubted you. I was only angry because of how much I care about you,' I told him. 'I just couldn't bear it if you didn't feel the same way.'

Aaron smiled and squeezed my hand a little tighter. 'Of *course* I feel the same way,' he said. 'I would *never* kiss you for a bet. I would only ever do it because I wanted to.' He swam closer still. 'In fact, I've thought quite a lot about whether I might get the chance to do it again.'

He leaned towards me. His face was so close we

were almost touching. I closed my eyes. This was it. At last, he was going to kiss me again. The moment I'd been looking forward to for days was finally—

'Emily! Aaron!'

I broke away from our near-kiss and turned to see what was going on. Shona was hovering in front of a bubble and beckoning us over. We swam across to join her.

'What is it?' I asked, trying to keep the irritation out of my voice. Did she know how long I'd been waiting for that moment?

'I saw something inside the bubble!' she said. 'It was really hazy, but it looked like me! I'm sure it was! It disappeared as soon as I'd seen it. Now it's just a misty, mushy bubble.'

'Take my hand,' Aaron said. We joined hands and the three of us surrounded the bubble. Shona placed her palms against it. Gradually, the mist vanished and an image came to life in front of us. Shona was right – it was her! She was talking to someone, a merman. I didn't recognise him. He looked a bit older than us, quite tall, very thin, with deep blue eyes, white-blond hair and a shiny green tail.

'Follow the tunnel,' the merman was saying to her. 'It'll lead you out.'

'What about you? Will you be OK?' Shona asked.

The merman smiled. 'I'll be fine.' He touched her arm and Shona blushed and flicked back her hair.

She started to swim away, stopping for a second to look back at him. He was still watching her. They smiled at each other again before Shona turned and swam away.

The image faded, just as the one of Aaron and Archie had done.

Shona's cheeks were pink.

'Who was *that*?' I asked.

'I have no idea! Surely he wasn't real? I can't believe I would've forgotten him!'

She looked around at all the bubbles. 'What *is* this place?' she whispered.

I still didn't know for sure, but I was beginning to remember. We'd been here before.

I reached for the crystal and watched as the colours flowed around it. The shimmering light was whiter than before, and stronger, *fiercer*. I could almost feel it humming in my hand.

Follow me.

'Come on,' I said. 'It's telling us to keep going.'

Holding the crystal out in front of me, I led the way. We swam down towards the very bottom of the lake, brushing the sand with our tails as we followed the crystal, lower and lower, deeper and deeper. It felt as if we were swimming towards a secret place, way below anywhere that anyone had ever been before.

As we swam, we passed more bubbles in all sorts of shapes and sizes. Then, suddenly, the crystal stopped humming. The light calmed to a soft white glow. We couldn't swim any further; a bubble was in our way.

We approached it and placed our hands on it. Immediately, the bubble fizzled away to reveal a technicolour scene. It was me – with some sort of sea creature.

'The narwhal,' I breathed.

Aaron turned to me. 'The what?'

'I-I don't know where that came from,' I said. I didn't know where the lump in my throat came from either, or the tears that were suddenly threatening to burst out of my eyes.

We waited for the scene to unfold, like the others had done, but nothing happened. Nothing much, anyway. There was just me and the sea creature. I had my arms round its neck. We were both crying.

And then, I don't know why I did it, but something made me let go of Aaron's hand and swim towards the scene, into the image itself. Still holding onto the crystal, I swam towards myself.

I held the crystal out in front of me. One of the sea creature's tears fell on it. So did one of mine. As they mingled together, the crystal burst into light in my hand. It was as if someone had poured petrol onto it and set it ablaze. I jumped back, falling into Aaron's arms.

The three of us watched as the lights exploded like a box of fireworks.

'I remember,' Aaron whispered when the lights finally calmed.

Shona looked at me, an expression of horror and recognition on her face. 'Neptune,' she said.

'He's in trouble,' I added. 'Or he was. Is he safe now?'

All three of us were suddenly armed with fresh memories – but I still didn't know what we should do with them. Luckily, it seemed as if the crystal did. It was glowing and bouncing in the water, spreading light ahead of us and straining to get away. It was like a dog on its lead, begging us to hurry.

Follow me.

The crystal led us to the tiniest crack in a rock, way down at the lowest point of the lake. We'd never have seen it on our own. It was only because of the crystal's light that we spotted it.

'Will we fit through there?' Aaron asked.

'Only one way to find out,' I said as I slipped inside the crack and slithered along, into the darkness.

'Where on earth are we?' Shona breathed. The crystal had led us to a clearing full of shining, glistening bubbles. They were different from the others. They didn't bounce and float. They just hovered, gently humming in tune with the crystal's own vibrations.

You have found my own memories. I left them for you in my tears. I hope they help.

The voice seemed to be coming from the crystal. It was a voice I'd heard before.

'It's the narwhal's memories!' I said.

Aaron held out his hand. 'Ready?'

I nodded. We chose the biggest bubble of them all. It was bigger than any of us. As I held Aaron's hand, all three of us placed a palm on the bubble. Within moments, the shiny surface dissolved against our skin.

I held my breath, gripped tightly on to Aaron's hand, and waited nervously to see what kind of scene was about to unfold.

Chapter Eighteen

*T*wo figures swam into view, surrounded by a misty glow.

I waited and watched as the mist cleared and the image came to life.

'It's Njord and Archie,' Aaron whispered.

'What are they doing?' Shona whispered back.

They were huddled together in a small cave, talking quietly. I leaned in closer to hear what they were saying.

'Are you sure it is done?' Njord asked.

'I'm positive. Neptune is finished. His memories

have been taken – along with everyone else's. There is just the child left now, and she will do as I tell her. By the time she comes back, we will be the only ones who know anything. You have put the spell on the narwhal?'

A horrible cold feeling spread through me. What were they talking about?

Njord nodded. 'It will only last the rest of today – but that's long enough. The creature will not be able to communicate with the child. So there's no danger that it will tell her of our plans.'

Archie smiled an evil smile like I'd never seen before. The only smiles I'd ever seen from him were the soppy ones he saved for Millie. 'Good,' Archie said. 'In any case, the thing will be dead within the hour.'

Njord grinned back at Archie. 'You have done good work,' he said as he slapped him on the back. 'You will be rewarded.'

'And my reward – it will be the one that has been promised to my family for generations?'

'Of course! Your family have been my most loyal spies for as long as I can remember. You are my right-hand man, and the best warrior I have ever had. As soon as we have killed my brother and flooded all the lands, the world will be divided up along new lines. All the new territories will be ours for the taking. And you, my friend, will rule over one of the largest.'

'Thank you, my lord,' Archie said. 'Now, I'd better get back. I don't want to make Emily suspicious.'

'You know how to act?'

'Of course. From now on, both of us must act as if we remember nothing.'

'Correct. But not for long. Tomorrow, we put our plan into action.'

Archie bowed his head to Njord. When he raised it, he was smiling again. 'My lord,' he said. 'I cannot wait.'

The image faded away.

No one said anything for a long while. What on earth *could* we say? The three of us just stared into the space where the image had played out.

Aaron recovered first. 'That did just happen, didn't it?' he said. 'I didn't imagine it?'

'It happened,' I said woodenly.

'And we're sure that it's a real memory?'

'Pretty sure. All the others we've seen have been real.'

Shona shook her head. 'I can't believe it.' She sounded close to tears. 'Archie! He's been the closest advisor to the king for years.'

'That whole story he gave us yesterday was a massive pack of lies,' I said, the memories flooding back now. 'Archie's not to be trusted at all!'

I could feel anger beginning to bubble away inside me, clearing the fog of confusion and shock. 'We need to get back to Neptune,' I said. 'We have to warn him – and quick. They're planning to do this today.'

'But how will we convince him of what we've seen?' Shona asked.

'We'll find a way,' Aaron said.

'We have to,' I added.

Without another word, we turned and swam up through the darkness, back through the lake, through the tunnel inside the mountain and out across the open sea, with just one aim: to find a way to convince Neptune of something that we wished with all our hearts wasn't true.

'I'm telling you, whatever you have to say to me, you can say in front of my brother!'

'But Your Majesty,' I insisted, 'it's something we really just want to share with you.'

Neptune frowned and shook his trident at me. 'Do not contradict me!' he bellowed. 'Njord is the only family I have. He is my nearest and my dearest. I will *not* have any secrets from him. How dare you even suggest that I might! And Njord feels exactly the same way.'

Njord grinned inanely and slung an arm round Neptune's shoulders. 'You and me – we're a team for ever, bro,' he said.

I thought I might be sick.

Aaron swam forward and tried a different tack. 'Your Majesty,' he began. 'Like you, we're obviously *delighted* to have your brother back in our lives. We look forward to the two of you ruling over us together.' He smiled a broad, convincing smile at Neptune. 'In fact, we are so excited about the reunion that we want to help you plan a special surprise for Njord – a *secret* surprise!'

Neptune lowered his trident. 'Hmm, ah, well, when you put it like that . . .' He looked at his brother for approval.

Njord casually waved a hand. 'Go, go, do it,' he said cheerfully. 'I love surprises!'

Finally, we managed to drag Neptune away from his brother. As soon as we were out of Njord's earshot, we lowered our voices and talked quickly.

'Njord can't be trusted,' Aaron said bluntly.

Neptune stared at him for a moment – and then burst out laughing. 'Oh, that's funny,' he said, slapping Aaron on the back so hard he nearly choked. 'That's a good one. My long lost, dearest twin brother, the one I've just been reunited with after who knows how long apart. The one I have spent the morning catching up with, making plans for how we will work together to rule the seas in harmony . . .'

Neptune's smile disappeared. He flicked his large tail and came closer to us, so close I could see bits of his breakfast on his beard and smell it on his breath. 'Don't you dare tell lies about my brother,' he growled. 'I will not have it. Do you understand?'

'Yes, Your Majesty,' I replied quickly. 'Of course we understand. We're very sorry. We were only—'

'We were only telling the truth,' Aaron said firmly.

Shona grabbed my arm. 'Look!' she hissed in my ear.

I glanced over to where she was pointing. Archie had approached Njord. They seemed to be talking seriously. Archie nudged a thumb over at us, and Njord frowned as he looked across.

Had they figured out what we were up to? Had someone followed us to the lake of memories earlier? Did they know we were putting on an act as much as they were?

They were making their way towards us.

'You *have* to believe us!' I said urgently to Neptune. 'Please! We would *never* lie to you.'

'And nor would my brother! How could you be so cruel? How *dare* you try to twist my mind with evil lies on such a joyful day?'

'It *won't* be a joyful day if you don't listen to us,' Aaron urged.

But it was too late. Njord and Archie had joined us.

'Everything OK over here?' Njord asked, all smiles.

I gritted my teeth. I wanted to swim right at

him and tear that stupid, lying smile off his face. I couldn't believe he had Neptune at his mercy like this. I couldn't believe he was going to win. And I couldn't believe that Neptune didn't realise that if Njord won, it meant that every single one of us had lost.

'Everything's *fine!*' I said, forcing my mouth into a smile as big as his. Two could play his game. 'We were just telling Neptune how pleased we are at the way things have turned out.'

'It's so exciting!' Shona said, smiling so hard I was surprised her eyes didn't pop out.

'Couldn't be more happy for you both,' Aaron added, again smiling so brightly that the three of us could have been auditioning for a toothpaste advert.

Njord frowned as he looked round at us. Archie stared right at me. I held my breath and held my smile and prayed that they believed us.

Then Njord broke out into his horrible grin. 'The children are right,' he announced. 'It is *wonderfully* exciting!'

Phew! We'd pulled it off. Now we just had to figure out how to force Neptune to listen to us before Njord and Archie put whatever they were planning into effect.

'In fact, it is so exciting that I would like to bring the party forward.' Njord went on. 'Why wait a moment longer?'

'Why wait, indeed!' Neptune agreed.

'Wonderful!' Njord said. 'Let's get the celebrations started straight away.'

'Straight away?' I gasped. What was he up to?

Neptune threw a dirty look my way. 'Sounds good to me,' he said, turning back to Njord.

'Give me half an hour,' said Njord. 'I would like to prepare a surprise for my brother.'

I bet you would.

'Ooh, I love surprises,' Neptune said.

'I'm pretty sure you're not going to like this one,' I whispered under my breath.

'What was that?' Archie asked.

'What? Nothing. Just saying that I love surprises too,' I said stiffly. 'Can't wait.'

'Well then, that's just *swishy*,' Njord said, with a smirk. 'Now, go fetch your other friends – Beeston, and that Millie person – and we shall meet back here in half an hour.' He looked round at us one last time, and with another evil sneer that I couldn't believe Neptune still hadn't noticed, he said, 'Let the celebrations begin.'

We were back at the meeting place at the top end of the fjord, just in front of the mountain range.

'This is exciting, isn't it?' Millie said from her boat.

Archie was in the water beside her. 'It certainly is, my darling,' he simpered.

'Now then,' Njord said, as we swam closer to the mountain range. 'There is a special and very beautiful place in a cave nearby. I believe it is the perfect place to begin our celebrations. Come!' He spread an arm out, showing us where to go. 'After you,' he said to Neptune, patting his shoulder with brotherly affection.

We started to swim down the fjord towards the cave.

Don't do it.

The voice was so soft I only just heard it. 'What was that?' I asked, spinning round to whisper to Shona and Aaron.

'What was what?' Aaron asked.

It's a trap.

Again, I only just heard it. It sounded as though it was coming from a long way away, or from inside a tunnel or something. 'That! The voice! Didn't you hear it?'

Shona shook her head. 'I didn't hear anything,' she said.

If they hadn't heard it, that only meant one thing. It was the narwhal! I swam harder and caught up with Neptune just as he was on the very edge of the cave. 'Please, Your Majesty,' I said, grabbing his arm. 'Don't do it – I'm begging you!'

Neptune looked down at his arm and shook my hand off. 'Don't do what?'

'Don't go in there. It's a trap!'

Njord swam over just in time to hear what I said. At my words, he burst out laughing. Neptune glanced at him, and immediately did the same. Then he looked more serious.

'I don't know why you are intent on spoiling this special day,' he said, 'but I will not have it! Do you hear me?'

I gritted my teeth. 'I'm not trying to spoil anything,' I hissed. 'I'm trying to *save* you.' I nudged my head at Njord. '*He* is the one trying to spoil things for you. I promise you. He's not what he seems.'

'I'm telling you, child,' Neptune said, his face growing red and his voice rising. 'I will not have it. You will not—'

She's telling you the truth.

The narwhal. Clearer this time. It sounded as if he was coming closer.

Neptune spun round. 'Who said that?'

No one answered. I fought down the hammering heartbeat that was jumping up into my throat, and in a squeak, said, 'The narwhal.'

'The what?' Neptune asked.

Njord swam right up into my face. 'The *what*?' he growled.

'The narwhal,' a voice behind us said.

The three of us turned to see a young merman

swimming towards us. As he got closer, I could see who he was. Seth! The merman who'd helped Shona and me escape from the mountain!

And he wasn't alone.

The narwhal emerged from behind him and swam straight over to Neptune. As soon as Njord saw him, his face turned white.

Njord pointed at the narwhal. 'You're meant to be dead!' he said before he could stop himself.

The narwhal touched Neptune's forehead with his tusk. Instantly, the whole place lit up with swirling colours, flying between the narwhal and Neptune and dancing in the air like a bouncing rainbow.

For a moment, everyone was so still that I actually wondered if time itself had somehow frozen. Neptune stared at Njord; Njord stared at Neptune; Archie stared at the narwhal; Mr Beeston stared at Archie; Millie stared into space; Shona and Seth stared at each other. And Aaron and I stared at them all and waited for the *serious* sparks to fly.

Which, approximately thirty seconds later, they did.

Chapter Nineteen

*n*eptune erupted out of the water and practically flew through the air as he made a grab for Njord's neck.

'You filthy, dirty, lying eel!' he bellowed. 'You double-crossing, vile piece of sea scum! How *dare* you try to trick me like this? Pretending to be my loving, long lost brother, when you are in fact my most sworn and hated enemy!'

Njord was still white with shock. He turned to Archie. 'What's the meaning of this?' he hissed. 'I thought you told me you'd sorted it.'

Neptune froze. Slowly, he turned to Archie. '*Archie?* My closest advisor?' he said in a shaky voice. 'You were part of this?'

Archie looked down.

'What, you haven't even got the decency to admit it?'

'*Decency?*' Njord spat. 'Why would he need decency when he works for me?'

Neptune carried on looking at Archie. 'Why?' he asked, almost in a whisper.

Archie finally raised his head to meet Neptune's gaze. 'I was always with Njord,' he said firmly. 'It is in my family's blood.'

Neptune made a kind of snorting noise. 'And what is your motivation? What false promises has he led you to believe?'

Archie held Neptune's eyes. 'He has promised me one of the largest areas of ocean to rule,' he said.

Neptune laughed drily. 'And you believe him?'

'I have no reason not to.'

'Then you are a fool!' Neptune said with a dismissive shake of his head. 'And he is welcome to you.'

I swam forwards. 'And what about me and Aaron?' I asked.

Archie looked down at me as if I was a piece of rubbish he thought he'd got rid of. 'What *about* you?'

'What was the *real* reason you wanted us to have Neptune's power?'

Archie looked at Njord.

'Tell them,' Njord snarled. 'What harm can it do now?'

'Njord had begun to melt,' Archie said. 'The midnight sun was slowly working on him. We knew that one day he would rule again. We were patient. We waited.'

'But then Neptune removed the memory drug and started remembering things,' I said.

Archie nodded. 'If he had remembered before Njord came back to life, he would have frozen him all over again. Njord would never have returned to power.'

'And you would never have been given your share of the spoils,' Neptune said bitterly.

'So where did we fit in?' Aaron said. 'You can't have thought we would be on your side.'

'*You* would never have known *whose* side you were really on. In case Neptune remembered everything, we needed to get you here before he came himself, get you to catch the water and melt Njord.'

'To do the very thing we ended up doing, in fact,' I said.

'As it turned out, yes.'

'Which was why you were so keen to escort them on the trip,' Mr Beeston put in.

'And why you wanted me to phone you and give you updates on exactly what was happening here,' Millie added through gritted teeth.

'And you'd have spun whatever pack of lies we would fall for, to make us do it,' I said. I felt sick to my stomach.

Archie shrugged. 'I was just doing my job,' he said. 'Everyone is loyal to someone.'

We fell silent for a moment as we digested everything Archie had told us.

Then Seth cleared his throat and swam forwards. 'Um, excuse me.'

Neptune had his head in his hands. 'Not now,' he said.

'Your Majesty, it's important.'

Neptune finally turned to face him. 'Wait, I know you. I remember you. You're—'

'Yes, I'm one of your spies. I have always been loyal to you. But we haven't got time for that now.' He pointed over his shoulder. 'It's Njord,' he said. 'He's getting away!'

We all looked to where Seth was pointing. He was right! What was Njord up to? He'd swum halfway down the fjord and seemed to be rising up from the water, lifting himself higher and higher. Holding his arms aloft and turning in a slow circle, he was talking – chanting something. The water around him was beginning to ripple.

Seth was still talking to Neptune. 'Your Majesty,

I'm sorry but I really think we need to—'

His words were, literally, washed away. Whatever Njord was up to, it was causing havoc with the water. The fjord's level had risen, and the sea was bubbling and frothing all around us.

Millie screamed from inside her small boat.

'Hold on!' I yelled.

Aaron battled through the foaming water to help her. 'Throw me a rope!' he yelled.

Millie threw a rope from the deck and, between us, we began to pull her away as the water grew fiercer.

'Where's Archie gone?' Neptune yelled to us.

I glanced round. 'There!' I said. He had swum over to join Njord. What were they up to?

You have to get away from here.

'Did you hear that?' I said to Neptune.

He nodded. 'Let's get out of here.'

We swam as hard as we could, battling against the currents and the whirlpools that had taken over the once peaceful fjord.

Hurry. Get to the open sea. You will not survive anywhere else.

'Swim!' I yelled to the others. 'Swim as hard as you can!'

We pelted down the fjord, Njord's laughter bellowing through the narrow passage and chasing us all the way down.

'Swim as fast as you like!' he called. 'You will not

stop me. *No one* can stop me now!'

My arms worked like a windmill in a cyclone. My tail spun like an aeroplane's propeller. All I could think was that we had to get away from whatever Njord was doing.

Eventually, we threw ourselves out of the end of the fjord into the open sea. Neptune led the way. After him came Mr Beeston, then Aaron pulling Millie in her boat, then me, and finally Seth and Shona.

Panting and breathless, we looked round at each other.

'All here?' Mr Beeston asked.

'I think so,' Aaron said.

Below my tail, the narwhal nuzzled against me. 'You're safe!' I breathed.

As safe as any of us are right now.

I shivered. 'What now?' I asked.

Neptune shook his head. 'I don't know.'

We didn't have long to wonder.

Millie was the first to see it. Lifting a shaking hand, she pointed back down the valley we had just swum through. 'L-look,' she stammered.

I turned to see what she was pointing at. 'But that . . . but that's . . .' I ran out of words. There was no longer a valley with a peaceful fjord and towering mountains on either side. The whole space was filled to the top with foaming, rushing white water, building higher and higher and rushing in our direction. It was bigger than any of the waves we'd seen so far. Bigger than any wave I would ever have believed could exist!

'The tsunami,' Neptune whispered. 'He's doing it.'

'Doing what?' Millie asked.

'He wanted to flood all the lands,' Neptune said, his voice coming out in rasping gasps. 'He wanted to turn the whole world into an ocean. That was the plan. That was how this all started.'

The wall of water was still building. It was taller now than any of the mountains, racing towards the end of the valley – and towards us.

'As soon as it hits the open ocean, it will build to unimaginable heights,' Neptune said frantically. 'And that will be the end of us – and the end of the world that we know. He has spent many, many years designing this wave. It will destroy every bit of land it touches.'

Seeing the speed at which it was travelling, I figured we had about thirty seconds to stop it – if that.

'Do something!' Shona yelled frantically.

Seth grabbed her hand. 'Your Majesty, can you defeat him with your power? Isn't it stronger than his?'

Neptune shook his head. 'I can slow the wave down, hold it back, but that only gives it time to build even higher. I can't stop it.'

'Please try!' I screamed.

Aaron swam to me. He took my hand – and as he did, the wave seemed to slow a little – and grow higher. It was towering over the mountains now, building into a white, foaming peak.

Go to Neptune. Hold hands. Surround him with your power.

Of course! We still had Neptune's power in our hands! Maybe between the three of us, we could be stronger than Njord.

I pulled Aaron over to Neptune. 'Hold both my hands. Make a circle around Neptune,' I said, panic making me efficient. 'Quick!'

Aaron did as I said.

Neptune glared down at us. 'What do you think you're—'

'We're helping!' I said. The water was coming closer. I could feel the wave's spray on my face. I shook my head and clung to Aaron's hand.

'Now, just think hard – all the thoughts you've got that can stop it!' I yelled.

Aaron and Neptune both nodded. I closed my eyes, held tightly on to Aaron's hands on the other side of Neptune and whispered quietly, 'Make the tsunami stop. Freeze it, turn it to stone, do anything – just don't let it happen.'

Over and over again, I whispered everything I could think of that might save all of us from being killed in a matter of minutes.

The first thing I noticed was the sound of a seagull flying overhead.

Wait – if I could hear a seagull, then that meant I *couldn't* hear the sound of millions of tonnes of rushing water, and *that* meant . . .

I opened my eyes. We'd stopped it! The sea was completely still!

'Aaron! Neptune! *Everyone!*' I yelled.

One by one, each of us rubbed our eyes and looked around.

'Where's Njord?' Shona asked.

Neptune nodded his head back towards the valley that moments ago had been full of a towering tsunami. Njord's wave was still there – except it had changed. It was no longer water.

It was a mountain. The highest in the range.

'He always said that he would be at the centre of his tsunami,' Neptune said. 'He boasted that it would be made from his very essence, and that he would propel it across all the lands. We didn't just stop the wave. We stopped him – for good.'

'And Archie?' I asked.

Neptune shook his head. 'I imagine he was caught up in the tsunami too, or perhaps he escaped. One thing I can tell you for sure – he won't come near me or any of my folk ever again if he knows what's good for him.'

'I'll second that!' Millie said, sweeping a hand briskly through her hair and putting on as brave a face as she could. 'I don't know what I ever saw in the man.'

Aaron swam over and swept me up into his arms. 'We did it!' he said. 'We really did it!'

Shona and Seth smiled shyly at each other. They were still holding hands. 'You helped us stop Njord,' Shona said. 'If you hadn't come back with the narwhal, we would all be dead by now – or trapped in a cave for ever.'

'It was nothing,' Seth said modestly. 'Just doing my job.'

Neptune swam to Seth. He took him in his arms and squeezed him in a tight embrace. 'It was a *good* job,' he said. 'Thank you. And now that Njord has gone, I imagine you'll be needing a new one.'

Seth shrugged. 'I guess so.'

'How does advisor to the king sound?' Neptune asked with a smile. 'A vacancy has suddenly become available.'

Seth grinned. 'Really?'

Neptune laughed. 'Really. You have more than earned it!'

'Thank you, Your Majesty!' Seth said, beaming. 'I accept your offer!'

'What will happen to the narwhal?' I asked, as he swam around in between us.

'The narwhal will come home,' Neptune said. 'With me.'

I felt in my pocket and pulled out the crystal. 'And this? What shall I do with it?'

'Keep it,' Neptune said softly. 'As a memento of the day we made the world safer, and a reminder of your bravery and loyalty.'

I didn't know what to say – which didn't matter too much as my throat was too choked up with tears for me to say anything, anyway. 'Thank you,' I eventually managed to croak.

Neptune turned to leave. 'Come, let's go home.'

'Wait!' Millie said. She was pointing at the mountain. 'I've seen this before.'

We turned and looked at the mountain. The icy peak that moments earlier had been frothing waves, the wriggling waterfalls that flowed in long, jagged lines all the way down its sides to the sea. That was when I realised – *I'd* seen it before as well. Or I'd seen a reflection of it. 'The mountain from the lake!' I said. 'The one that we saw reflected but didn't exist in real life!'

'It certainly exists now,' Aaron said.

It was always meant to exist, I thought. This had *always* been Njord's fate.

'I don't know about any reflection in a lake,' Millie said. 'But this is the one I told you about.

The crying mountain from my dream.'

'Crying mountain?' Mr Beeston asked.

Millie pointed at the waterfalls. As I looked, I realised she was right. The sun glinted on them, lighting them up with tiny dancing rainbows. They would always flow, now. Njord's tears, falling into the sea and fading away – just like all his evil plans.

'At least he got his wish,' Neptune said softly. 'He can watch over the oceans for ever now.'

We stayed a moment longer, each of us lost in our own thoughts. Mine centred on how close we'd come to a very different ending.

I felt a shiver wriggle through me. I didn't want to think about that – I didn't want to think about any of it any more. It was time to leave it all behind.

I flicked my tail and glided through the still, blue water. 'So,' I said, shuffling closer to Aaron as we swam along side by side, the sun heading slowly towards its soft midnight glow as our small group headed slowly home.

'So,' Aaron said.

'So you mentioned something about maybe wanting to do something again. Something you'd done once before . . .'

Aaron smiled at me. 'Did I?' he asked innocently. 'I really don't know what you're talking about. What might that have been?'

I glanced at the others to make sure no one was watching. Mr Beeston was in the boat with Millie, rowing her along. Neptune was ahead with the narwhal, leading the way. Shona and Seth were behind all of us, talking and giggling as they swam. No one was looking our way. To be honest, at that point I didn't care, anyway.

'This.' I stopped swimming, grabbed Aaron's face in my hands – and kissed him.

When we finally came up for air, Aaron smiled the best smile ever at me. 'Oh, *that*!' he said, wrapping his arms tightly around me. 'Thanks for reminding me.' Then he pulled a face, a wicked glint in his eye. 'The only trouble is, I've got quite a bad memory,' he said. 'I might need reminding again. Maybe a few times.'

I pulled out of his arms and took his hand as we swam on. 'Don't worry,' I said, laughing as the happiest feeling I'd ever known bubbled up inside me. 'I won't let you forget.'

Shona and Seth were smiling as they caught up with us.

'What are you two laughing at?' Shona asked.

'Oh, you know,' I said. 'Just how to practise remembering things.'

Seth nudged his head back to where we'd

come from. 'Quite important really, considering where we've come from.'

I shivered as I thought about the lake of lost memories.

'Good point,' Aaron said. 'Maybe we should start practising right away.'

'Mm,' Seth said seriously. He looked at Shona. 'Maybe we should practise, too?'

Shona gave Seth a playful shove and swam ahead. I broke away from Aaron's hand and joined her. We flicked our tails, spraying water in Aaron and Seth's faces.

'You can if you can catch us!' Shona squealed, giggling as she splashed.

'You're on!' Seth replied.

With that, the four of us swam and raced and played for the rest of the day.

And by the time the midnight sun moved across the sky to bathe the ocean in its gentle light, we had made so many new memories that there wasn't room for all the old ones any more.

Thoughts of giant waves, evil brothers, stolen memories – or even crying mountains – they were nothing more than a drop in the ocean.

As always, lots of people have been involved in helping to make this book come about. I would particularly like to thank . . .

My family, for fulfilling their usual roles of first readers, proofreaders and general supporters along the way;

Dominique Royle, for enthusing about the midnight sun and insisting I visit Norway;

Lowenna Hughes and all at St Ives Travel, for organising the best research trip of my life;

The Hurtigruten ship, *Midnatsol*, for being absolutely stunning and amazing, and for providing ten days of incredible inspiration;

The Scattered Author's Society, in particular Celia Rees and Kath Langrish for one of those Charney lightbulb moments;

Lucy Coats, for the Bardic journey which led to Njord's poem;

Amber Caraveo, for being a brilliant editor and for making the editing process such a creative, exciting and pain-free journey;

Lisa Milton, Fiona Kennedy and everyone at Orion, for being the perfect home for my books, and for doing so much to support them, and me. And Laura Tonge, for being a bit of all the above, and more.

Girl next door. Best friend. Mermaid.

The Tail of Emily Windsnap

Can you keep a secret?

I know everyone has secrets but mine's different. I mean, how many mermaids do you know?

It all started with a swimming lesson at school. I was in for a big surprise, and, after that, the surprises just kept on coming. I discovered a whole other world beneath the waves and found a new best friend.

This is my story.

Swishy wishes,

Emily Windsnap

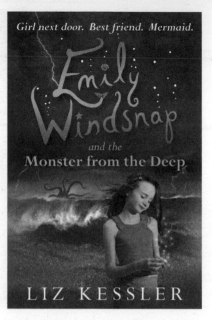

Emily Windsnap and the Monster from the Deep

Here I am at last, on a beautiful island in a glittering sea – a place where human and merfolk live together, and where it's OK for me to grow a mermaid's tail in the water. You'd think everything would be going swimmingly, but, while we were exploring, Shona and I stumbled on a sleeping monster – and I woke him up!

It was a monster mistake! Of course, I was determined to fix it, but could I?

Swishy wishes,

Emily Windsnap

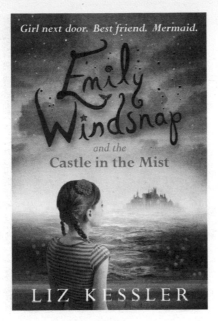

Girl next door. Best friend. Mermaid.

Emily Windsnap

and the
Castle in the Mist

LIZ KESSLER

Emily Windsnap and the
Castle in the Mist

When I found a ring buried in the sand, I couldn't resist trying it on. I didn't know it would drive King Neptune into such a rage that he'd send my boat spinning across the ocean. Luckily my best friend, Shona Silkfin, was there to keep me company. We wanted to know the story of the ring and the secret of the magical castle that we could see shimmering in the mist. Wouldn't you?

Swishy wishes,

Emily Windsnap

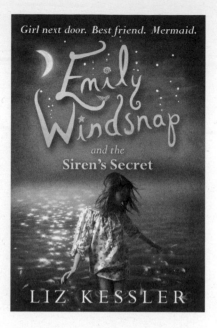

Girl next door. Best friend. Mermaid.

Emily Windsnap
and the
Siren's Secret

LIZ KESSLER

Emily Windsnap and the Siren's Secret

Do you ever feel like you're going crazy?

That's how I was feeling after our return to Brightport. Everthing seemed perfect but deep down I knew something was wrong. When I was thrown out of mermaid school, I decided I would go in search of the sirens, banished by Neptune to a top secret undersea cavern.

And when I did, I discovered an amazing story . . .

Swishy wishes,

Emily Windsnap